A DAY AT THE BEACH

and Other Brief Diversions

A DAY AT THE BEACH

and Other Brief Diversions

To Uncle Walt,
who plussed my life.

Acknowledgements

THIS BOOK WOULD NOT EXIST without the efforts of my wife and partner, Jill Q. Weiss, who created the cover and designed the interior, as well as editing the stories and consistently encouraging me. If you enjoy these brief diversions, say thanks to her.

Special gratitude goes to Dr. J.T. Sparkles for awesome critiques and honesty, as well as her professional use of emoticons and emojis.

My hard-working and diligent barista friends at various Starbucks through the years need to be recognized. Their pleasant attitude and friendly greetings make starting the day easier. The eight-pump venti soy chai tea makes getting through the day better still. These little stories are just long enough for a coffee break.

There are three groups that I must mention as well. The annual madness called the Southern California Writers Conference, the monthly fun of the Southern California Writers Association, and the random brushes with greatness of the Orange County Screenwriters Association are each wonderful places to meet and greet folks at all stages of the process and the business of writing. The people I meet at these events are eclectic, talented, and very supportive. I have learned so much and have a lot more to learn.

No writer works in a vacuum. Every author is the sum of many parts. The books we read are a critical element to the perpetual growth of a writer's craft.

Gene Wolfe once told me, "If you want to be a good writer, read good writing." You cannot read better writing than Gene Wolfe's. Thank you, sir.

Author's Notes

THE MOST COMMON QUESTION authors of speculative fiction get is, "Where do you get your wild ideas?" I myself was privileged to ask a very famous science fiction/fantasy author that same question when I was too young to know that it was not a very smart question to ask. His, no doubt pithy, answer is lost to my faulty memory, but it was something like, "The drugstore."

One of my beta readers asked me, "Where did you get all the wild ideas for these stories?"

"Everywhere," I replied.

- A young woman, walking past an independent coffee shop, accidently steps out of her shoes. Seated at a small table on the sidewalk, a younger man watches and does not laugh.

- "Can you write a story about anything?" asked our friend Karen. "Yes," I replied. A song comes on the radio. Watch out. You might get what you're after.

- Falling asleep while watching an episode of "The Prisoner" and waking up to a documentary on celebrities who died young, the thought arose, "What if they didn't die?"

- Multiple viewings of Aladdin the Musical made me ponder, "What would a genie wish for if he held a second lamp?"

- Standing in line behind my wife in a large department store, a woman asks, "Are you waiting in line?"

  "Yes," I reply. "Why do you ask?"

  "Well you don't have a cart, or anything in your hands." She is bold.

  "The truth is…" I begin lying, "I just like to stand in lines. I figure that if I stand in enough lines every day I will meet everyone I ever knew and then we can apologize to each other for all the hurt we may have caused."

  Deep inside my mind I wonder, "Where do you get this stuff, Jeff?"

- Some friends depart. What if I never see them again? Were my last words to them worthy?

Ideas are easy. Making a cohesive story is not so easy. Unless…

Sometimes the idea is so good that the words just pour out of the author's brain and heart onto the page. It is that way with the stories in this book. Almost. Once the basic story arrived in raw form it needed to gestate, develop, mature, and mellow until the rough became smooth and the facets gained polish and luster.

The temptation to say, "That is good enough," is very strong. A writer owes his readers more than "good enough," however.

After the initial publication of this book, I found myself unhappy with several key elements, most notably the end of "Djinn," which I wrote as kind of an ongoing threat from the creators of the lamp. It was a distinctly unpleasant and unsatisfying ending. I like the new version much better.

In addition, several of the stories initially included were not of similar caliber or tone as the others. Not bad stories, mind you, just not right for the mix. So now, some are gone. Some are new. All are re-edited and enhanced.

Except "Small World." In my eyes that one is pretty perfect.

Table of Contents

Introduction

OSCAR WILDE ONCE TOLD ME, "A picture has no meaning but its beauty, no message but its joy. That is the First Truth about art that you must never lose sight of. A picture is a purely decorative thing."

The stories contained in this book are first meant to entertain. They are also, hopefully, thought provoking in a light way.

It is not my intention to preach any kind of message. The ideas in these tales are not meant to be taken as a belief system.

They are a way to pass the time. If they give you a different perspective on life and living, that will be a bonus. If they bring you some measure of joy, their purpose will be fulfilled.

Oscar never did tell me the Second Truth about art.

Jeffrey J. Michaels

A Day at the Beach

ALICE WALKED THREE STEPS before she fully realized that she had stepped completely out of her shoes. She turned and walked back to them before she became aware that her T-shirt had likewise left her body.

The sidewalk was not particularly crowded, but plenty of people were walking up and down on that beautiful day. A cool breeze blew in off the ocean and the pier carried many tourists out to Ruby's for a tourist meal and a tourist view of Catalina Island. Alice covered herself with her arms the best she could as she chased after her shirt, floating to rest on the sidewalk.

A part of her mind already worked on the problem of how she could lose her shirt. The shoes were a possibility, but shirts don't just fall off. Another part of her mind was shutting down in embarrassment. It wasn't that she didn't like the way she looked. Alice worked out at 24-Hour Fitness gym three days a week. She looked good, bikini good. Somehow, it was different being seen in a bikini top on the beach and being caught on the street in your bra.

Then she noticed that no one was moving. It wasn't that they had all stopped to stare. No one moved. No walking, no talking, no skateboarding or bicycling or cars or sound from Java Town coffee shop or anything. She stood quite still and slowly looked around. No one moved.

With a sudden sweeping motion she bent and picked up her shirt and slid gracefully into it, pulling it down, tugging at the hem to test its security and then, as an afterthought, tucking it into her jeans. Which weren't there.

A kind of mad feeling grew somewhere inside, an "Am I going crazy?" kind of fear. She spun back to where her shoes still lay and there between her and the shoes were her jeans. From somewhere far away she noted that they were still zipped, snapped, and belted.

"It happens like that." A voice came from nearby. "Hold still a minute. You haven't completely synced up."

Alice looked around, not really registering her surroundings. She did not take the voice's advice. A man's voice, she thought in that part of her brain that still tried to make sense of this. Picking up her jeans, she went to work on the fastenings.

A young man stood up from a wire chair near a wire table. Others sat there as well, but they did not move. No one moved. Except the young man.

Well tanned, dressed in shorts and flip flops with a hooded sweatshirt, hair curled slightly and naturally and light in color. Not tall, but taller than Alice. She was tall for a girl. He smiled a little and said, "Try to hold still."

She held her jeans in front of her as he walked over and stepped past her a bit. He bent down and retrieved her bra from the ground. She looked down quickly and felt relief that her T-shirt was still on her body.

"Lotsa questions I know, but really, just hold still for a few minutes. It gets better. Trust me." His voice stayed soft and he looked directly into her eyes.

She felt scared. Trust did not always come easy for her, but her brain told her that maybe, this one time, she could trust a stranger just a little. Her brain told her that it did not have a clue as to what exactly was happening. The man in front of her wavered a little.

He didn't waver back and forth, he wavered in her vision as if she had lost his signal, like the cable TV went out for a moment or she went through a tunnel and her cell phone wavered. Alice squinted at him.

"Sorry, did I waver? It happens. If you move real slow you can try putting on your jeans. I'll look up, but it's best for me to be a little still right now too. So, I won't turn around, I'll just look up, okay?" He tilted his head back and squinted at the sunlight high in the sky. Slowly he lowered his sunglasses from the top of his head over his eyes.

Alice didn't bother giving her approval. She did snatch her bra from his still outstretched hand. He wavered in her vision again.

"Slowly," he said.

Slowly she slid the jeans on and slipped back into her shoes. "So…uh, what's going on?" she asked.

"Don't know, really." He snuck a quick peek and looked back upwards when he saw that she was still buttoning her jeans. "Um, you might want to wait a while before you try putting on your uh, your…" Alice smiled a little as she noticed him actually blushing, "the rest of, um, your, uh, clothes." Alice went to put her undergarment in her purse and realized it too was missing.

"Where'd my purse go?" she asked, turning about quickly. She spied it lying back a ways beyond where her shoes had been and started to walk that way.

"Wait!" he said. She froze, but noticed that her shoes were no longer on her feet. A quick check to see that shirt and jeans were in place and then she let out a scream, "What is happening to me?"

"Please, just hold still! It gets better, I promise." He moved slowly around in front of her again and handed her panties to her.

"Are you doing this?" Her voice became very intense and she directed it at the young man. "If this is some trick I'll hurt you! I'll kick you! I'll punch you hard and I can! I've been practicing!" She had balled up her fists, one undergarment in each hand, and was threatening him.

"No. No! It's not a trick, really!" His voice in turn was pleading. "I'm stuck here just like you are! Have been for a while. Like I'm in between, we, we're in between. It's like time stopped, sort of…I don't know, really I don't. It's not my fault. Please. Just hold still a bit. I'll tell you what I know." Alice still felt a little crazy and knowing that her clothing might…well it wasn't falling off, exactly.

"Why won't my clothes stay on?" she demanded.

"You're phasing. It happens to everyone." He seemed a little relieved that she was calming down. He raised his sunglasses back to the top of his head, pushing against his curly hair.

"What do you mean 'phasing'? Who's 'everyone'?" Her eyes were narrowed, but she had lowered her fists.

"It's a word I use. I don't have any idea really what is happening. I just got the word from a Star Trek show or somewhere. I've been here, 'in between,' a long time. Could you, could we, just talk? Just calm like, you know, talk?" He patted the air between them with his hands. He looked tired and worried and a little like a puppy that had gotten lost. He actually hung his head.

"Sure, let's talk." Alice dropped the intensity in her voice. As long as she didn't look around she could pretend that this was just another slightly clumsy attempt by some guy who wanted to meet her. If she looked around and saw that no one was moving...

Seeking some measure of control Alice said, "Let's start with your name and then I'll tell you mine, okay?" She ducked her head a bit until she caught his downcast eyes. He looked up and smiled. "And then you'll tell me what's going on, right?"

"Right! I'm Charles." He stuck out his hand. Alice smiled at the weird formality of it, but returned the gesture and said, "I'm Alice."

When their hands touched she felt as if she would faint. Charles quickly got his arm around her shoulder and helped her to a seated position on the sidewalk, exclaiming, "Sorry, sorry, sorry," over and over.

"I forget about that part. Look, as best as I can figure out, somehow time has kinda stopped for me here. It's like I fell between the seconds or something and I'm always here, in the 'now.' Every now and then someone else sort of falls between too. Until they completely adjust, it's like their possessions don't quite follow their movements. It freaked me out for a while when I first, uh, arrived or whatever. I kept running around and suddenly I was streaking. After a while it stops happening, but you gotta take it slow."

"So why did I feel like I was passing out when we touched?" Alice looked a little pale.

"Um, you weren't grounded," Charles said dubiously, "or something. Look, I don't have any science answers here. I call things what sounds right to me. So I think when I touch one of the newbies it's like they get pulled further into this, um, the between."

"Great. So now I'm here and I can't get back?" Alice was rethinking slugging him.

"No, people go back all the time. As far as I know I'm the only one who can't get back." His voice got soft. She decided to try to be calm. Taking a deep breath she stood and looked him directly in the face. Alice liked his eyes.

"Blue," she said.

"No, I've gotten used to it."

"No, my favorite color. It's blue, like your eyes." She was flirting and she didn't know why. Charles blushed. "So, what do you do for fun in, uh, in between?"

"Well, for one thing, everything is open and everything is free. But it's no fun going to a movie. The actors just stay still like, well…" he waved his hand around, indicating the people staying still on the street. "Do you want a latte? I can make one of those for you. I learned how."

"Sure. So the coffee makers work, but everyone is frozen?"

"It is weird, but things seem to work fine if I'm near them. Just not people. Or animals. Here, can you stand okay? Let's walk slow. We gotta use Java Town, 'cause Starbucks is too crowded. Sometimes I can get cars to work and I watch TV a lot over at Best Buy. Not cable, but DVD's. They'll probably be pissed at all the movies I've opened up, but I'm not stealing them. I've borrowed some box sets from Barnes and Noble, but I always put them back. We could watch a movie if you want."

"Charles, this is really strange and you're what? Asking me to go with you to a movie?" Alice was having a hard time again. Charles had walked behind the counter and began making her a latte. Two girls were back there with him engaged in a frozen conversation. One had her hands spread out and appeared to be saying something like "As if!" while the other blew a pink bubble with her gum.

Charles turned back to Alice and saw where she was looking. "Sometimes I think about popping her bubble," he said.

"Why don't you?"

"Karma."

"What?"

"You know, karma. If I pop her bubble maybe something bad will happen to me."

"I don't really think that karma works that way and you're trapped between seconds. What could be worse?"

"Oh, it's not really that bad. At first maybe. I've gotten kinda used to it. Just gets lonely, that's all. Sorry about the movie invite. It's been a long time since…" he paused a while looking into her face, "since a girl was here. Never in fact. Just some older women and some guys. Most of them freak out right away and never get over it. I do my best to get them to slow down and just stay still, you know, live in the moment. They get scared. Like they're gonna miss something if they don't get back. I try to tell them, nothing will change, but they're in a hurry mostly."

"I'm scared. A little." Alice took a breath. "I am. I'm scared, Charles. This is not normal. People don't just stop moving or have their clothes…" She pushed her lips together in frustration. "People's clothes don't just 'phase off' their bodies!"

"Actually everyone is still moving, just real slow. And don't be scared. I'll help you get back."

"How?"

"Well, I'm not sure how it works, but I think if you don't get too used to being between, you don't actually sync up completely. One day you just sort of speed up or maybe it's slow down and then you're back."

"How do you know?"

"Roger."

"What?"

"Roger, over there." Charles pointed to a man that was standing near a surfboard display on the sidewalk. "He was my best friend for a while. He knows the lyrics to like every song. Then one day he just went back. I still talk to him sometimes."

Alice looked at Charles with narrowed eyes. "You talk to him?"

"I like when you do that, with your eyes. You have nice eyes. Warm, deep. It's not like he talks back and I'm not crazy, like I think he hears me or something. Just lonely. I'll probably talk to you when you go back, um, just talk." He turned and started the steam machine, drowning out any further conversation. When he finished steaming the latte he turned and asked, "Are you hungry? I can get us some food. Later I'll show you how to get a bed to sleep in; just let me know when you get tired."

Alice sipped her drink. It was really very good and she told Charles so. "Well, I've had a lot of practice," he responded.

"How long have you actually been between, Charles?"

"Don't know, really. It took me a while to kind of get a structure to life at first. There's nothing to tell me the passing of time unless I wear a watch. They have some nice ones here and I wore some of them for a while, but the day just is always about two o'clock. I think it was six minutes to two when I first went between. Recently I heard a long droning noise. It took me a while, but I think it's the clock across the street tolling the hour.

"I know it's been a long time subjectively. I learned that word from a book in the library. I watched all of the episodes of Xena and Hercules and when I figured out how much time it took it was like three weeks or something. I've watched a lot more TV seasons since then. A couple of years. More actually.

"Once I drove to Sedona in Arizona. Once to Seattle. Gas pumps work if I wait a bit and stand still and close to them. Get my 'field' around them or something. Sometimes the food on the grills is hot. Fruit in the stores stays fresh. My iPod works and my computer. Even the internet sometimes, like Wikipedia and stuff that is always the same. No e-mail though, no IM-ing."

Alice looked at him in disbelief. Years? She had things to do!

"I have things to do! I can't stay here for years! I have to get moving! I have to get..." She realized that she had started to scream again and struggled to gain control.

"Hey, it's okay. It's okay. It's gonna be okay." Charles' voice was calm, his eyes sincere, and the light in them helped her attain a level of steadiness. "C'mon, let's get out of the coffee shop and go to the beach for a while. It always helps."

They walked out the door and turned left towards Pacific Coast Highway. Charles walked right out into traffic. Alice had lived in Huntington Beach for about seven years and knew the rules about crossing PCH. You hit the button on the stop light three times and stand back and wait for the walk signal. Everyone used the walk signal. "Stop!" she screamed.

"It's okay! Really, c'mon." Charles danced in the road a little. "I'll have to learn to be careful again if I get back, but really, everybody's stopped. C'mon, you'll feel better at the beach." He turned and skipped a step and twirled and waved for her to follow. Alice stepped gently into the flow of halted traffic.

Together they walked down the steps near Duke's Restaurant and around a low wall onto the wide, nearly empty beach. It was a weekday, Wednesday, and late in the season, September in fact, and the latter part of the month and turning two o'clock and Alice fixed all these things in her mind as she walked past a volleyball game.

A muscular young man was frozen in a futile dive towards a ball hitting just inside the line. A plume of sand rose around him, arcing from his feet into the air. The sand hovered above the beach. His teammate, a young woman, crouched in a posture of frozen dismay, her face contorted in a state of denial. Her mouth stretched open and it looked like she was saying, "Noooooooooo..." It looked like she had been saying it for a long time. On the other side of the net another young woman, pretty with hair so blond that it was almost white, hung in the air mid-jump, hands and arms raised in victory. She wore a pretty knit cap pulled down tight over her head and her hair wisped out from the edges. She wore a pink bikini and Alice noticed an onlooker staring at the girl. Her partner was just landing near the net, his arms still raised from the volley return, his face opening up in a way that revealed that same sense of victory. Alice looked at a scene of action and movement and nothing was happening. They were frozen in a balanced state of defeat and victory.

Alice felt a hand on her arm and jumped a little. She had stopped to stare at the tableau. Charles' hand pulled her along. "C'mon," he urged her quietly and she allowed herself to be led away.

They got to the water's edge and Charles stood in front of her. Taking her face gently in his hands he looked very intensely into her eyes. "You need to release some energy. It will help. It always does and I don't know why. Screaming is good. Try screaming."

Alice didn't need any prodding. She let loose a scream right then. Charles fell backwards. Alice kept at it, stopping only for breath and, then, not that often. She did aerobics. Her lung capacity was good.

As she screamed she felt the tension draining away. The ocean had been frozen, waves neither rising nor falling. Out about forty yards a surfer had gotten to his feet as he caught a wave. A little farther away another wiped out. Neither one moved. As Alice screamed, the water near the shore lapped a little in small ripples and waves. A soft sound came to her ears, like the sound of the ocean in miniature. No other sounds could be heard. Trembling, Alice sat down in the sand.

Charles was settled in and calmly waiting for her to finish. "Thanks," Alice said, "I do feel better. That probably wasn't all that pleasant for you though. Sorry."

"Nah, I kinda liked it. I don't get to hear many living noises." He stared out at the sunlight now sparkling off the little waves. Further out the waves remained still. They sat in silence. Alice's stomach growled loud enough for Charles to hear.

Slightly embarrassed, Alice said, "I can't be hungry, I just had lunch." She made a show of patting her stomach as she turned and looked at Charles for the first time since she screamed.

"No, it's been a while," he said matter of factly, "maybe five, maybe six hours."

"No, it can't have been that long. I don't believe that. I don't sit still that long. You must be wrong." She protested and chided him for a moment. Without looking at her Charles said, "Look at your watch." Her watch read seven thirty-nine p.m.

When she had finished screaming again Charles said, "So, are ya hungry?"

They established a little pattern over the course of her first days between. Charles found her a house that she liked, one that he knew to be a vacation home over on Seventh Street and near Pecan. It looked clean. There were new sheets and blankets. He taught her how to stand still near the shower head until the water started to flow. It took a while for the temperature to regulate, but eventually she learned to step in and out and not turn the water off.

"It's probably a good idea to stay close to where you first fell through," Charles explained. "We can get some of your stuff from your apartment, you know, some clothes and, um, personal items. Make it easier, more normal for you, until, well, I think if you stay close to where you came through you'll get back faster. Maybe."

The day was beautiful and endless and they spent a good deal of time near the beach and walking the pier and eventually she took him up on the invitation to a movie.

Charles was a good companion. He cooked and walked and helped and talked and listened. He listened really well.

He looked at her while she spoke and asked her questions and encouraged her to share her innermost thoughts. He constantly assured her that she would get back, that she wasn't missing anything, that nothing would happen without her. He would get a little wistful look when he spoke like that and Alice could see the loneliness of his future.

Together they read books. Together they wrote little poems. Together they laughed and pondered and asked deep questions on the nature of humans in the universe and silly questions about cartoon characters who didn't wear pants versus those who do. Never did they ask about each other's past. Alice tried once or twice and Charles made offhand little jokes and quickly changed the subject.

He let her pick out a movie one day, night, moment…they were never able to decide what to call the time that they were at. Alice had tried for a while to keep track of days, but that fell apart quickly. There was just no point.

She chose *Somewhere in Time* with Christopher Reeves, a time-travel romance tale. They enjoyed their first kiss at the end of the film. After that, Charles let her pick out the movies most of the time. She usually chose ones that he wouldn't watch on his own. Once, after they'd watched the entire set of Tracey and Hepburn romantic comedies, he stayed the night, day, sleep period.

Charles seemed younger than Alice. He had no need to be focused on his life and when she asked him what he would be doing with his future, he just stared off and shrugged.

Sharply focused, Alice had many irons in the fire of career building. Sometimes she would open her day planner and review the appointments that she was going to have to keep eventually.

Charles would just laugh a little. "It's always the same day," he would say.

They had very different ways. Charles wasn't the kind of person Alice would ever have been interested in before. She would not have taken the time to know him. Here, in the relaxed area between seconds, Alice and Charles fell in love.

They drank good wine. They had fires on the beach. They walked and talked and just held each other. They went to museums and gardens and the libraries. Once they were at the Central Library long enough that one of the fountains started to splash. Charles was deep into a book. Alice was reviewing notes for an important meeting. A short distance away, another fountain started to flow.

"Now that's funny," she said, looking around. "They've never all started to run at the same time…" Alice looked at Charles and saw him waver. Charles looked at her with tears in his eyes. Together they reached for each other. Then, Charles held back.

"Charlie." Alice's voice was a plea.

"Quick." Charles moved towards the bikes they had been using. "It happens fast."

He left her no choice but to follow. He rode back towards the beach. She wanted him to stop, to talk, but he just said over his shoulder, "Quick." He didn't look back.

Charles wavered in her vision several times as they sped to the corner where they first met. How long ago? She pedaled faster when she thought she would lose sight of him. They arrived in what seemed to be good time, but there was no way to tell. Now they dropped the bikes on the sidewalk and turned to each other.

She realized how much she loved him and tried to tell him so, but he would have none of it. She would move on, he told her, and there was no guarantee that they would ever see each other again. Well, Charles would see her, but that was it, they would never be together. Alice reached for him again. Tears left his blue eyes and trailed down his face.

She had so many questions for him at that point. What did he want her to do? What was he going to do without her? Who was actually leaving who? How can she help him? How can he get back to where life was real? She got angry that she had not thought to ask these things before. She got angry with Charles because he didn't seem to want to return with her. He actually stepped away from her…and then the clock finished striking two.

A car alarm blared nearby and the clatter of a skateboard swiftly approached. The ocean roared and the traffic roared louder. Overhead a plane roared and nearby a man roared in laughter. Everywhere people were moving and talking and gesturing and laughing and yelling and the cacophony was overwhelming.

Alice stood stunned in the middle of the sidewalk. Nearby she heard a man say, "Charles?" It was Roger and he turned around, looking very confused. She kept reaching out...but Charles...he was gone from her sight. Alice felt her breath come in a gasp, her chest felt constricted, her stomach turned.

A young woman wandered by calling, "Charlie! Charlie, where are you?" Her eyes wide, she looked at Alice and said, "I can't find my little boy. He is curly blond with blue eyes. Have you seen him?" Alice did not, could not reply. The woman took a sharp panicky inhale and cast her eyes about the street. Before Alice found any words, the mother of little Charlie had turned a corner and vanished. Alice gasped another breath.

In a state of disbelief Alice moved quickly towards the beach. Maybe he had come back later. Maybe he was waiting for her somewhere, somewhere special. She ran down the steps that she and Charles had walked up and down countless times. She ran to the beach and saw the many well-worn tracks of their footprints leading past the volleyball game to the sea. She saw that the game had continued and the girl in the hat now dove for the ball. Everyone laughed and shouted, urging her to success or failure depending on which side of the net they sat. The sand that she kicked into the air fell back to the beach.

Alice hurried to the water's edge and saw the waves crashing regularly onto the shore. The surfers had all paddled back out and were waiting for the next wave. Some were paddling into an oncoming swell. It was quieter here, but the noise of the ocean filled her mind. She felt like screaming. Instead, she wept.

The next few hours blurred past. People talked to her and she couldn't understand what they wanted. Alice canceled all the appointments that she had made for that day. She lost a big sale and nearly lost her job.

Her boss called her in later that week and told her that she had lost her edge, that she needed to tighten up her act and get her momentum back. He just didn't understand what happened to her. Alice agreed.

It didn't help that in her first hours back she opened her planner and found several long, hand-written letters from Charles tucked in different pages. Each had a number on it. He gave instructions that she should read them one a day or one a week or perhaps one a month.

She read them all in one night, her first night without Charles. Later that week she opened the trunk of her car and found a packet of letters there as well. She went home and searched her closets and drawers and found letters from Charles hidden in many places.

Hurt and angry she wondered, how could he do this to her? Why would he create these constant reminders of their inability to be together? Why would he treat her this way?

She read every word he wrote.

"Dear Alice," he always began the letters this way. "I have looked into your eyes often since you returned. I dream that somehow you can see me."

"Dear Alice, I kissed you ever so lightly today. I miss your voice."

"Dear Alice, I just returned from a trip to Chicago. Actually, I lived there for a while. It is a beautiful city and I hope you will go there someday and think of me wishing you were there."

"Dear Alice, I just returned from living in Atlanta and some other towns. People seemed to be moving slightly in those places and I wanted to see if, perhaps, I would see you moving again. Nothing in Huntington Beach has changed much. I wanted to kiss you. Instead I cried and said good-bye."

"Dear Alice, I spoke with you today. I told you that I would be leaving town again for a long time. I will travel the coast down south into Mexico and maybe farther. I tell you this because I may not return to our hometown and I want you to know that I still and will always think of you and remember you."

"Dear Alice, it has been many years for me and for you it has only been minutes. I found you near the ocean. You have moved some distance since I went to Peru. Alice, I went into the Andes and lived for many years. The people I met there can walk between! I learned so much from them, but when I return here I still cannot find my way back to you."

"Dear Alice, I know that, right at the end, just before you returned, you tried to ask many things. You sought some meaning for this experience you and I had. You may be thinking that you should wait for me to return and, I confess, at first I would have wished for this to be true, something that you should do. Now, I am different. I have seen so many things and been alone for so many things. I believe I may not be the person you knew. I do not know exactly how this all will work. You will read these letters over the course of many months, but they come to you over the course of many years, decades perhaps, of my subjective time. Please, whatever my outcome, return to your life. It is a great gift. Enjoy every moment. I have."

"Dear Alice, most beautiful woman of my heart and days. Of all the experiences in my life, you have been my best."

"Dear Alice…"

And then one day she could find no more letters.

She stopped at the place on Seventh and Pecan, her home from between, and there, wrapped nicely, was the clothing and books and papers and anything that belonged to her that she had moved into the dwelling. A note on the top read, "I turned off the shower." Alice laughed at that, for the first time since…since she had seen Charles last. His letters told her that he had done so much, lived so many experiences. It had only been a short time from her perspective, only a few days. He seemed to have grown so much. She started to feel happy for him.

*****

After the second week of being back, she started to hit her stride again. The tears stopped flowing as constantly and the drive to succeed returned.

She rarely visited the beach after that and she moved from her small apartment into a house she purchased further inland. Investments were made. Goals were achieved. Money flowed and her life looked good to others. She was promoted and headhunted and made an offer and she negotiated and got stock options and a package and within a short period of time achieved everything she had set out to achieve. And she felt empty.

Two years later Alice accepted an invitation to a business luncheon at Duke's Restaurant next to the pier in Huntington Beach. The man sitting across from her, a very high-powered, impeccably-attired business associate spoke of goals and profits and retirement at thirty-seven. He looked Alice in the eyes only occasionally and when he proposed to her, he couched it in the terms of a merger and used words like synergy and paradigm. Alice said she would take the offer under advisement and really did not know exactly what she meant by that. He shook her hand and gave her a peck on the cheek as the valet pulled his car around. He tipped the exact percentage and drove off without looking back. She found she could not recall the color of his eyes.

The valet stood patiently by as Alice looked in her small purse for her ticket. She stopped and excused herself and said she would return in a little while. All through the meal she had watched the waves of the ocean from their table on the veranda. They seemed to be beckoning her, reminding her of a different way, a different time. She walked slowly out onto the pier and all the way to the end.

A pod of dolphins attracted the attention of a group of tourists. Sleek and smooth, they slipped in and out of the ocean. The water played across their bodies when they surfaced, droplets dancing between sea and sun. Watching as they rose and dove between the waves, Alice stood very still.

The day grew quiet. Slowly she became aware of an elderly man standing quite close to her. She turned and he smiled.

His eyes were her favorite color.

Small World

"WALTER?"

"Yeah Mick?"

"Let's get out of here."

"The apartment?"

"No. Here. Let's get out of *here*. Off Main Street. Away. Let's go somewhere."

"Like?"

"I don't know. New Orleans maybe."

"We can catch the train. I'll get Lilly Belle…"

"No, I mean the real New Orleans. In another state."

"Well, the real one is under water now."

"Really? What happened?"

"Hurricane."

"What is that?"

"Weather. Bad weather."

"Really? What is bad weather?"

"You know, like rain and wind, except a lot of it and it doesn't stop for a long time."

"Can't they just sell a few ponchos? Go inside and shop a while?"

"It is different. They all had to leave. Now they have to clean up and repair."

"So New Orleans is closed?"

"Sort of."

"We could go see the Matterhorn, the real one. Maybe climb it? Or see a real castle?"

"Our castle is real. Besides, you need a passport. Then you have to have another photo I.D. to get through TSA."

"I've got my annual pass. It's deluxe!"

"They are very specific, Mickey."

"Africa? We can see real hippos! Or piranhas!"

"Um, piranhas are in South America. Different than Africa."

"But they are together on the Jungle Cruise."

"It's just a ride, Mick. Besides, real piranhas eat mice. It wouldn't be safe."

"Not safe?"

"Nope."

"Well, maybe we should just go get a Monte Cristo, see the pirates and the ghosts. That's safe, right Walt?"

"That's safe. Just the way we like it."

Burning Down the House

"IS RAMMING THAT MACHO ASSHOLE'S TRUCK part of the new me?" Tina looked at her canine companion and said, "Once for 'No' and twice for 'Yes.'"

"Yip." The dog looked at her and then away.

"You're sure?"

"Yip! Yip!"

Tina's Highlander was full, but not stuffed. It still smelled of pine and nature. It held everything she needed. Scaling back felt good. All her life in one vehicle. That was the goal and the trip north was the test.

All her life and Byrne, the dog.

Now Harrison's big Ford truck blocked her drive by just enough to be annoying. She allowed a regret. Why did she ever get involved with that macho asshole? Deep breath. Exhale. Regret gone.

The truck was on the street because that macho asshole was grilling in his driveway. Harrison, of course, was nowhere to be seen. Gouts of flame leapt from the Weber grill. Always lighting fires and moving on. Reckless.

His grilling always charred the meat, everything well done and too hot. He used too much lighter fluid. His food tasted like fuel. A plastic container of Kingsford fire starter sat open on the ground, way too near the flame. Cocky and dangerous.

Well, those were the reasons she allowed herself to get involved with him. Playing it safe all her life had not gotten her what she wanted. Harrison ignited a passion inside her and it burned away her old notions of propriety. Macho asshole. He knew nothing of propriety. He lit fires and moved on.

Deep breath. Exhale. Regret gone. Again.

The month she just spent at a cabin near Yosemite was nice. Cool and moist, the forest growth lush and verdant. Her time there proved she needed nothing from the past. Her past. She felt renewed. She felt different.

The solitude had left her with only herself. Well, herself and Byrne. It isolated only who she was now. The hiking gave her thoughts motion. The climbing gave her perspective. Chopping wood for the hearth fire made her feel strong. She'd lost a lot of weight and gained a lot of muscle with all the physical activity. It was not just calories she burned, but also bridges. Mentally at least. Emotionally too. It strengthened her for some difficult conversations. It was time for some physical bridge burning.

Now she needed to re-enter her old home, confront her past one more time. Confront her sister and her stuff. Their parents passed away almost six years ago. Since then, they stored all of mom and dad's old stuff in the garage of the little townhouse they shared. Tina wanted none of it.

Sister Chrissie wanted it all. They compromised and Chrissie got her way.

The townhome in Huntington Beach was supposed to be an equal share between them. It was equal only in the way that they had always been equal. Chrissie got her way. Always. And Tina took care of her little sister by giving in. Again and again. Tina started to seethe. Deep breath. Relax. Release.

She looked at her hands and up to her arms. Tan now and not so burnt. No longer pale and pasty. A month of being outdoors and solitary did what nearly twenty years of living the bar scene at the beach had not.

"You would think," she said to Byrne, "given the geography, that I would have been tanned all my life."

The dog blinked in the bright Southern California sunshine and said, "Yip, yip."

She pressed the button that opened the garage door. It was a futile gesture. She could not get in the driveway. She could not get in the garage if she did. Two packing boxes fell off a stack. A third teetered precariously. The fallen boxes popped open and the contents spilled down the slight slope of the short driveway.

One held salt and pepper shakers, her mother's collection from her travels around the country. Somewhere there was a box of tourist spoons to match.

The second box split open and sent eight track tapes skidding across the concrete. Eight tracks! Inside the other cartons were magazines bound in bundles, old school papers and report cards, photos of people she never knew. All combustible.

Tina noted that she had not yet turned her vehicle off. Could she just leave? Her thought lingered and then connected with her voice. "Could I just leave it all behind? Could I just leave?"

"YIP! YIP!" Byrne the dog was a rescue. Bright-eyed and intelligent, sister Chrissie brought her home from the shelter where she once volunteered. Typically, the volunteering had not lasted long. Responsibility for caring for the dog also had not lasted long. Responsibility never lasted long in Chrissie's world.

Byrne gravitated to Tina. Byrne was smart. She knew where her food and walks originated. Chrissie did not even seem to notice the shift in allegiance.

Tina ran a mental examination of what was in the SUV. All her financial and legal documents pertaining to her life and the property: deeds and wills, birth certificate and passport, stock portfolios and insurance policies, all were packed in a locked fireproof box tucked safe beneath everything else she owned that she needed.

She actually owned more. It was all inside that overstuffed townhome. She owned more than she needed.

Thirty-six, Tina thought. Sister Chrissie is now thirty-six and does not need me. And I do not need her. "I don't need my sister." The words came out on an exhale. Tina looked at Byrne. "Do I need anyone? Do I need you?"

Byrne stayed silent, but looked Tina in the eye. "Once for 'no.' Twice for 'yes.'" The dog turned away and looked at a nearby patch of dry grass. "My own decision, is that what you mean?"

"Yip, yip."

She noted the dog's glance. Cutting the engine, Tina secured the parking brake and climbed out of the Toyota. Byrne followed swiftly, light on her feet and agile. The dog hit the grassy area in a hurry.

Tina stood listening to the sounds of the neighborhood. Somewhere kids laughed. Somewhere seagulls screeched. Somewhere a TV played too loudly.

Actually, that came from inside the house, her house. Chrissie laughed too. And another laugh, *a macho asshole laugh*. Had they not heard the garage door?

Screeching car tires, a hail of bullets, and fierce subwoofer-driven explosive noises sounded down to her ears from the 5.1 sound system Harrison installed for them.

Another laugh. Harrison.

And then another sound. Chrissie.

And then Harrison.

Animal sounds of heated passion.

Tina felt her skin go hot with anger. No reason could she find within her brain for such heated anger, but she let the fury rise anyway. Her world seemed to sway.

Byrne was at her side just then. The dog looked around and whimpered just a little. Agile and light, Byrne jumped back into the Highlander.

The earth jolted. Once, then again, and followed by a long rolling motion.

Tina fell on her rump and watched the trees shake. Dry leaves scattered down from dry branches. More boxes tumbled from the garage.

Harrison's truck bounced and rocked on its tall tires.

Chrissie screamed as the earth moved.

The flaming Weber grill fell over. The lighter fluid spilled. A rivulet of fire was flowing toward the dry Southern California grass separating the two driveways.

Tina stood up as the earthquake subsided. She watched, mesmerized, as the fire devoured the small parkway. She watched the wind blow the embers. She watched sparks dropping all about the scattered boxes. She felt the wind on her face and stood still.

"Should I stay or should I go?" she asked aloud.

Byrne whined.

"Not a yes or no question is it?"

"Yip, yip."

Tina looked at the encroaching flames. "Should I stay?"

Byrne looked at the fire.

"Should we go?"

"YIP! YIP!"

Tina climbed in her Highlander, took a deep cleansing breath and hit the ignition.

Resort Island of Lost Souls

THE NOTE READ, "DIAL 369 WHEN YOU AWAKE." That was all Michael knew for certain. That and one more thing. He felt terrific. Better than ever. His hands explored his nose and face. He smiled. Everything felt better than it had in years. Even his hair felt good.

He stretched his limbs in the long bed. They did not ache, but seemed stiff. "How long have I been asleep?" His voice sounded rough, but only from disuse. He cleared his throat. "Where exactly am I?" He spoke to no one, but somehow the sound of his own voice made life more real.

To one side, a nightstand held a glass of water, the note, and a phone. He gratefully sipped the water. It was icy. Michael dialed. Immediately a voice came on the line.

"Hello! So happy you are awake. There is a shower and toiletries if you wish to clean up. In the closet is a set of clothes. Later we can help you personalize things to your needs. Call again when you are ready for the tour." A pretty voice, not girly, not boyish, but light and mellow. A kind voice.

Michael did not take long getting ready. Curiosity drove him, his mind clearer and more active than it had been in thirty years. Only the recent past was fuzzy. He seemed to recall agreeing to come here, but where was here? There was no anxiety about his situation, only a feeling of relief.

He made the second call. A gentle chime signaled the door. A woman, slender with cool blue eyes smiled, holding out her hand to greet Michael.

"I am Grace. I will be your guide today. You have many questions and it is my responsibility to give you the answers you need and deserve." The voice was the one from the phone.

Michael hesitated slightly at the handshake. Looking down at his naked palm and fingers he saw no blotchiness, just a smooth cocoa coloring. Grace started to draw back.

"I am sorry. Perhaps you wish to avoid physical contact?"

"No." Michael enjoyed the sound of his own voice, clearer still, the pitch in the upper registers, vibrating high. "No, I am just…well, it all seems different today somehow." He held out his hand and gave Grace's a gentle shake. He felt as if he should bow. "Where am I exactly? I think I wanted to be here, but I can't remember much of anything."

"With your permission, why don't we walk about a little? I will explain as we go. They say it is important for you to get mobile, get your legs moving."

"Get mobile? I feel marvelous!" Michael did a little step and then slid backwards and twirled, arms in the air and fingers snapping smartly.

Grace caught him as he spiraled towards the floor. "Gracious! Did that make you a little dizzy? It was really quite marvelous! But you have to build up to it, alright? You have been still for a while now. Do not worry, everyone goes through this stage."

Michael sat on the floor. Grace held him by the shoulders. "Okay, I'll take it slow, but that felt great!" They laughed together and slowly rose to stand. A short walk took them to a doorway. Grace handed Michael a pair of dark wraparound sunglasses. "You will want these. I guarantee it." Donning her own pair, she swung the door open. Bright sunshine filled the hallway.

Grace touched the outside of the door. "This is door number six. If you get lost, just tell anyone that you are in number six. They will bring you back here. We will get you a more permanent address when they are happy with your strength."

"Who is 'they'?"

"Well, they are sort of like doctors, but different. They help you get better, but not by cutting you up or putting pharmaceuticals in your system. They have technology that regenerates your cellular structure. You will do fine. You went into the process in pretty good shape, I understand. Your muscles were toned. They kept you there a little longer because of some brain stuff. I do not possess all the details. They will meet with you later, maybe tomorrow, and answer those questions for you, alright?" They walked together a short way. Grace stopped and pointed regally towards a vista of sand and sea.

"Oh, how nice! Look down by the boat!"

Michael did look and saw the boat, tied up at a dock in a small bay. Several people were gathering there, some with guitars.

"I think you will like this. Are you strong enough to walk, or shall I call for a cart?"

A long, sloping walkway wound from the door down to a beach. Palm trees and flowers covered the land between the curves. Michael raised his line of sight and looked about. A series of terraces went up a gentle hill. The top was not far away, but the pathways roamed to and fro. Several buildings stood just at the crest, but only one structure, a domed tower, appeared to go above the top of the hill. Roofs and parts of walls showed through the foliage, but never an entire building. Other people wandered and strolled about.

A red and white striped vehicle pulled up a few steps away from the door. Grace said, "Well I guess we are taking a cart! Hello, Walt!"

"Hi Grace. I hear our newest citizen is alert and ready for a tour. Do you mind if I join you?" Michael looked at Walt and blinked in disbelief. He seemed just like…

"You do not mind if Uncle Walt joins us, do you?"

Still stunned, Michael said, "No, that'd be great. I thought that…" he stammered a little, "I mean, didn't you, um…"

"I know I said you should move your legs a little. It's okay. You will get plenty of exercise in the next few days. It isn't often that we see Uncle Walt. This is quite an honor." Grace spoke the last words in a stage whisper with her hand against her face. Michael climbed aboard the vehicle at her invitation.

Walt spoke as he drove along the flower-lined paths. "Grace, I think what our friend Michael is really wondering is how can I be here? Well let me tell you a little story, Mike. It all started in the 1930's. There was a lot of scientific exploration happening then and a lot of discoveries being made. Some folks made a great deal of money developing these inventions. I made quite a bit of money myself.

"A war broke out. There was some concern about the world at the time. We didn't know if it would survive some of the science being developed. A few of us got together, informally at first, and we started asking questions: crazy, sky blue questions. We started to get ideas. The ideas didn't always go along with the thinking of the governments.

"We began a quiet program that took the best minds into a sort of secret society. Some kept on developing the weapons and the drugs the governments required from them. On the inside, they kept thinking differently. Certain funding for other projects got funneled into our ideas.

"During the war we discovered that we needed a private place to work. We couldn't just disappear, however. Some of the scientists decided to arrange their own deaths. It was a bigger world back then, not so much technology designed to observe the planet.

"We found places in jungles and deserts to set up labs and facilities. But no one really wanted to live in a jungle or a desert. So we developed certain…well, we called them 'resorts' and actually ran them as such. People could come and stay like they were on vacation. All the while, research was going on in hidden rooms beneath the hotels and restaurants.

"After the war, we expanded them into high class places in the Caribbean, the Mediterranean Sea, the Alps, certain lodges in the National Parks of the United States, some islands of the Pacific and, of course, my favorite was an orange grove in Southern California.

"We were a serious bunch most of the time, but every now and again we needed some entertainment. We expanded our roster to include those, like yourself, who may be involved in the arts or entertainment. The first person to come our way was Glenn. He had grown tired of touring and playing the same songs over and over. One day his plane vanished. Or that is what the world thought. It is unfortunate that we didn't have the regeneration technology in place before he grew older and died. I miss him quite a bit." Walt paused and sighed.

"Others followed over the years for similar reasons. Grace herself was weary of constant public attention. So was Diana. You will meet her by and by. We thought you might be ready for the same thing, so we contacted you. You may not recall everything yet, but it will come back to you soon. The amnesia is short term, but your mind needs to be awake to completely activate. Well here we are at the boat."

Michael looked out and saw that the boat was actually made of concrete, an extension of the stone dock. A group of musicians gathered there, playing little riffs and snatches of tunes. Some sounded familiar. Others caught Michael's ear and made him want to hear more. A man with dark curly hair sat near two women.

"Cass, try it this way." He didn't quite plead with her.

"Jim, it won't work that way. Look, you are a good singer, but I know harmony." She wore a bright yellow dress with large flowers printed on it.

"I don't think he's looking for harmony," said the second woman. "He's looking for an effect. Are you sure you were a rock and roller?" She laughed a cackling giggle and held the back of her hand to her mouth.

"Janis, Cass can do anything she wants, but I think Jim is right." A deep-voiced man joined the conversation, slipping his guitar into playing position and turning to Cass. He ran strong, long fingers across the strings.

The man addressed as Jim leaned forward. "Oh, that is good, Jimi. Play it again."

"So you really don't want a note, you want a noise?" Cass leaned against Jimi and he placed a little kiss on her cheek.

"Not a noise. A sound, Cass. Janis' voice is too bluesy. I need smooth noise…I mean, sound." Jim demonstrated what he meant, but stopped. "See, I can't quite get there. It's out of my range."

"Something like this?" Michael spoke up and let out a little trill and soft noise somewhere between a scream and a hum.

"That's great!" Jim jumped up. "Do that again! Jimi, do that little lick." They started in together. Cass and Janis sat still until Jim went through a couple of verses and sang a chorus. They joined in and made a unique harmony of their rough and gentle voices. Not rock, not blues, not jazz, but something new.

Michael turned and saw Walt and Grace smiling. "It'll be good having you here, Michael!" They waved at the musicians and drove away toward the tower at the top of the hill.

Djinn

"SO, CAN YOU JUST HANG OUT or do you have to live in the lamp?" The young man ran long fingers through his blondish, curled hair.

"I grant wishes. When I am not engaged in this activity, I must merge with the lamp." The voice emanated from within a slowly coalescing cloud of reddish smoke. A head and torso were visible as were muscular arms, crossed at the great chest of the red-skinned being.

"So, do you want to be in the lamp?" The young man looked up at the creature that had recently emerged from the antique his mother found in her travels.

"I am not actually *in* the lamp." The being was now about eight feet tall, mostly a column of smoke, not showing any signs of lower limbs or even a pelvis. His tone of voice shifted from pronouncement to lecture, and vague annoyance at the question.

"Okay. That doesn't *actually* answer my question but, if you're not *in* the lamp, where do you *actually* go?"

"Do you not have a wish? You get three wishes." The jinni sounded puzzled. His voice again lowered in volume and he furrowed his red-skinned brow. His bald scalp wrinkled from back to front. Squinting his eyes, he looked again at the person holding the lamp.

The young man set the lamp carefully upon a picnic table. Afternoon sun gleamed from the single untarnished swipe where he had rubbed the cleaning cloth. He turned to the jinni and said, "Dude, have a seat if you want. Chill. Let's talk a bit. Is that okay? Is that part of the rules? A little conversation?"

"Mmmm...yes," the jinni said as he pondered the question. "I believe that conversation is within the guidelines."

"So?"

"What?"

"The lamp. Where do you go?"

"Oh yes. Is it your wish to go there?" The jinni's tone increased again.

"Nah, you smoking trickster!" the young man laughed. "I don't want to go there. I don't want to change places with you. I don't want unlimited powers. I'm just, you know, making conversation. You've been trapped in there for what, like a thousand years or something? Do you have a telephone or radio? Is there any way you can talk to someone? I'm just thinking you must be lonely. I figure you might want to stretch your legs a little before we get down to the three wishes thing. Um...do you have legs?" He looked downward below the djinn's torso.

Smoke swirled about the lower portion of the djinn. He also looked down. Large and reddish with a human shape, the djinn felt he was losing his air of power and command at the odd onslaught of odd questions. This human, the one who now possessed the lamp, the one he would now call "Master" until released from his servitude by the performance of his magical duties, was not asking *for* anything. In fact he seemed to want to know *about* the djinn. He seemed to be concerned with the djinn's comfort.

"I had legs," the jinni said thoughtfully, "once upon a time. I think they are still there, but I am rarely out of the lamp long enough for them to form."

"Ah ha! So you *are* in the lamp!"

The djinn scratched at his short beard. It was the only hair on his head and followed neatly the outline of his strong square jaw. The smoke from around his head and neck was fading, but clung to his shoulders and chest in wisps. He brushed at it absently and the wisps were wiped away.

"No. Not in. I go *in* the lamp, but it is like a portal, a gate. I move from here to there. I actually live on the other end of the portal passage." He moved his massive red hands about in circles and spirals. Bits of smoke trailed from finger tips. He wore two large coppery bracelets on his wrists, tight to his skin and smooth, polished. The smokiness was diminishing and the young human could see that the jinni was wearing a wide leather-looking belt which secured loose, flowing material below his waist. There were still no legs apparent, but the hint of pants gave conceptual solidity to the belief that they may yet appear.

"So why do you come here?"

"When someone opens the portal I am drawn here."

"Yeah, but why? Why do you do this? Is it fun for you? Are you a philanthropist?"

The djinn thought a moment. "Philanthropist..." he said, sounding the word out aloud.

"Do you know what that means?"

"I will. Just wait a moment." He looked upward and squinted at the bright sun. A breeze pushed at the smoke and made the loose fitting pants ripple. The jinni's face brightened and something like a smile broke wide across his face. "Ah, there it is! It takes a while for the language of the Master of the Lamp to fully emerge within my brain," he explained. His tone of voice returned to formal lecture mode. "No! Not a philanthropist! Far from it, actually. I am a prisoner. This is my sentence. My retribution. Generally, I do not like it. The people I meet are often greedy and selfish. They care nothing for others and think only of their own wants. You will probably do the same thing." He crossed his mighty arms and sniffed at the air. He dropped his voice to condescending and dismissive. "By this time they have wealth and power and sometimes fame, sometimes other humans to serve them. I am usually back in the lamp in minutes."

"Through the lamp."

"What?"

"You said 'in' the lamp. You meant 'through,' right?"

"Yes. Yes, through the lamp. Yes." He sounded annoyed and squinted at the human. "What is your wish, Oh Master!" The djinn's subdued tone once again rose until his voice reverberated across the deck like a subwoofer's vibration. Party lights shook and plates and glasses danced on the picnic table.

"Dude, take it down a notch!" The young man involuntarily stepped backward a pace.

"Is that a wish?" the jinni asked slyly.

"No, just social advice, man!" The young man again ran slender fingers through his longish hair. Curly and thick, it tumbled around his eyebrows and earlobes not unlike the smoke that swirled about the djinn. He waved a long, sunburned arm towards the picnic table and benches. Several comfortable looking chairs sat to the side. "You want to sit down? You want something to drink? Some lunch? Do you drink or eat? I got some food grilling. I can throw down another burger or two if you're hungry." The human looked his peculiar guest up and down. The djinn, broad and muscular, stood nearly eight feet tall. The boy eyed the plate holding the raw patties. "Or three or four."

"Eat? Drink? I haven't tasted food in centuries. What is 'burger'?" The mystical djinn smoke continued wafting away from him, merging with the smoke from the meat already cooking on a little Weber grill. Some of the meat smoke found its way upwards to the djinn's recently materialized nose. He blinked, sniffed, and then swallowed. "Yes, I would like something to drink. Do you have anything fermented? Or some pomegranate juice, perhaps?" The djinn's voice lost its basso profundo quality, becoming a little higher in pitch.

"Fermented? Dude, try this out!" The young human opened a bottle of beer and handed it to the djinn, who sniffed at the opening and then took a swallow. And another. Then a swig and in short order brought the empty bottle down on the table with a loud THUNK!

"Thank YOU!" The djinn spoke loudly, but not in the 'wish is my command' tones he used at first appearance.

"It's called Smoke Ale. They make 'em in Oregon. Want another? Try the Hazelnut Brown. Have a seat, man." The djinn lowered his large torso onto one of the long picnic benches. It bowed slightly under his enormous bulk and red smoke curled up through the spaces between the planks of the table top. Red lips smacked together as he quaffed several more bottles while the human grilled a number of burgers, setting them on buns in front of the djinn. The young man showed him all the condiments. The djinn took a liking to Ray's Barbecue Sauce.

Several burgers and bottles later he said, "Dagon be praised!" The djinn wiped his lips. His eyes were wide and his mouth stretched in a bright smile. Huge white teeth shone brightly against the reddish-hued skin.

"So do I call you Genie, or do you have a name?"

"A name?" The djinn paused in his consumption of burgers. A smear of sauce graced his right cheek, but was nearly invisible against his ruddy skin. "I had one. Once."

"Like legs?"

"Legs?" The djinn looked down at his legs, recently materialized. Faint wisps of smoke still clung to his ankles and feet, but there was definite solidity below the wide belt. "My legs!" he shouted with delight. Wide shoulders spread, and thick, muscular arms winged outward from his body. His hands were loose and fingers fanned open. Sparks, like miniature lightning bolts, shot from the tips.

"Cool," the young man said as he took a long pull at a fresh bottle of Dead Guy Ale, watching the sparking bits of energy fly about the wooden deck. A loose bolt struck the fabric of the canopy shading the table.

"Oops. Sorry," the djinn said, making a circular motion with one pinky finger. The fire he started dissipated, along with the scorched fabric. No evidence remained of the tiny conflagration.

The boy said, "I'm Adam." He was still watching the area where the djinn's hands shot lightning, mentally debating the wisdom of offering to shake hands.

"What? Oh, yes, names. My name. You know, this is very unusual. The lamp masters never really seem to care about me personally." The djinn sat still a moment and said, "On either end, actually."

"You say your name is Adam?" The djinn squinted and little flashes of lightning sparked from the edges of his eyes. He looked a little fierce. "I knew an Adam once upon a time. Before the lamp. Long before."

"Well, probably not me. Heck, there's been lots of Adams over the centuries. We had five in my high school class."

"That many?" The djinn appeared to make a conscious decision to remain calm and the little sparks of lightning faded away. "There is much in a name. At least there was once."

He bent over, looking closely at the lamp on the table in front of him. Battered and rather unattractive, the coppery antique was tarnished over most of the surface. A short swath of gleaming metal showed where the young man started his polishing efforts. The djinn gazed at his distorted reflection. "I have not had to remember my name for a very long time." He scratched at his beard again, clearly puzzled. "I am sure I know it…"

"Dude, what name would you like to have?"

"What?"

"I mean, if you can't recall your old name, maybe you aren't that guy anymore. What do you think your name should be now? You know, who are you currently? What is *your* reality?"

The djinn did not know where to go with that thought. "I have been in servitude for so long. I imagine I would have to take a slave's name. My reality is based on what others request of me. They speak and I perform a task or duty."

"Sounds like where I work, man." Adam squinted in the bright southern sun. His skin was also red, though from sunburn. "You know, my name is Adam, but for a while I called myself Cliff. A few years back I was having problems with The Mom and The Dad and I just didn't want to be their son anymore, you know? So I spiked my hair up and wore black and told everyone that my name was Cliff. I thought it was edgy." Adam laughed. "Edgy. Cliff. Get it?"

The djinn sat still, staring at Adam. With no mirth he replied, "Cliff. Edge. Yes, a play on words. Good."

"Yeah, well then I got a job and some responsibilities and suddenly The Mom didn't seem so square that I couldn't get along and The Dad read this book by that I'm Okay, You're Okay guy, Dwayne Wire or something, you know, that bald guy on PBS." Adam glanced at the jinni and his bald head. The djinn looked upward as if to see his own scalp. Their eyes dropped back down and the two looked at each other, not quite embarrassed, but also not amused. "Anyway," Adam continued, "suddenly he's all mellow and chill and we're reading *Tao Te Ching* together, so I figure, long black pants and heavy black shirts are pretty hot here in California and the spikes made it really hard to sleep and, uh, do other things in bed, if you know what I mean, so here I am.

"What I mean is that I *decided* that I was Adam and that I didn't need the entire attitude. I am the one who gets to decide what the name Adam is about. I stopped looking outside of myself and started coming at life from within, y'know, my true self.

"And life got good. Deck, sun, beach, brews, and babes, man." He smiled to himself and then asked, "So, when was the last time you enjoyed the ladies?"

The djinn carried a wistful expression. "I think I recall a son once. Maybe several. And daughters too, now that I take the time to think about it. And Measerah. My wife, Measerah." His voice trailed away and his shoulders slumped forward. His chin dropped until it touched his chest. Puffs of pale yellow smoke rose from the sides of his face.

"Dude, so sorry to harsh the moment, man." Adam got quiet. They sat in silence for several minutes.

"Why do you call me that? Why do you say 'dude' or 'man' when you address me?"

"Well, that's just like a general title, you know, like for friends that aren't really your friends yet, because you don't know their name or if you, like, forget their name sometimes or it's just, I don't know, like a general nickname or something."

"Is it a sign of respect?"

"Respect?" Adam laughed a little. "Not always, man. It depends on how you say it. Mostly it is a sign of friendly. Like, 'Dude, we're friendly and it's all good, man.'" The young man rubbed his sandy hair. "Dude, what do they call you when you are *through* the lamp?"

"There is no real language used. They summon and I have no choice but to appear. It is the same with the lamp. It is a power. I am connected to the power, but not in control. I am its servant. Whoever possesses the lamp has access to the power but only through one who is born to it and lives within it. In this instance that one is me and the possessor is you. You can access this power three times only." Sensing a return to familiar territory, the djinn's voice was resonating again and he sat taller.

"What if I don't use it?" Adam asked.

"What? Why would you not use the power? Everyone wants the power." The djinn seemed perturbed at the mere suggestion.

"I don't know, man. I've heard stories about power. It corrupts. I got it pretty good right now. I'd hate to lose this." Adam waved a hand about, indicating the deck and house.

Silence descended. The djinn just stared at Adam. The boy started talking again. "Does it all revert to you somehow? I mean, I've got the power now, but what if I choke on a pickle or something? What if I choke and croak? What if I never get the chance to ask for something? Does it all time out somehow, or is it something I can give to someone else?"

"This," the djinn stroked his beard, "has never come up."

"What if I gave the power back to you? Do you get to set yourself free? I mean, what would you do if *you* got the three wishes?"

"They are commands, really. Your wish becomes my command. I labor to shape the energy to fit your vision." The jinni spoke the words, but his thoughts were slightly distant.

"Dude, that's awesome! But how do you know if it fits the person's vision? That's gotta be a pretty precise wish that they utter."

"True. Many are...imprecise in their command. Things often go awry in the fulfillment phase."

"Dude, did you just say 'awry'?" Adam snickered. "That fulfillment phase must be where the shit hits the fan."

The djinn sat silent, head tilted like he was listening to something far away. Adam's slang language grew inside his mind. Comprehension became awareness and the djinn's wide mouth spread in laughter. "Yes, yes. It is often better to call it the 'hits the fan phase'! Yes, brilliant words! Most expressive!"

Adam laughed then too. "So if you were making the wish *and* fulfilling the command, you'd get pretty precise, right? Most of the time you're on one side of the fan and the wisher is on the other, right? It's different if you're on the side where the fan flings the fulfillment."

The two of them laughed at the image Adam conjured. The djinn wiped at his eyes and said, "Yes, I imagine so. Ah, Adam. You are a different sort of Master of the Lamp, that is certain, but I am enjoying you. I have not had such talk for a great many eons. I will miss you when we are finished."

"Dude, why not just hang for a while? Do you have a time limit to complete the task? If I'm the Master then I set the pace, right?"

"That is a true statement."

"So if I gave you the power, you could set the pace, right?"

"I believe that also is a true statement, as far as it goes. Though I do not know if I can have the power outside of being a servant to it."

"So what if my first wish was to give you the power to do what you wanted?"

Silence fell yet again. When he spoke, the djinn's voice was very soft. "You make my head move in many different directions."

"Dude, that's probably just the beer. You need a rum drink and some bananas and pineapple. Wait here, I'll get you some fruit." When he returned, Adam held a tray bearing a huge Tiki-styled glass filled with a colorful golden-orange fluid. Speared on a long wooden stick were a variety of fruits, mostly citrus. The tray also carried a big fruit bowl. He set the tray on the wooden picnic table and handed the glass to the djinn.

Adam sat down by the bowl and continued carving up a pineapple that already had a few chunks cut out of it. A few other fruits fell to the slicing knife and Adam revealed a small plate of cheese hiding behind the fruit bowl. The two sat together quietly while the djinn took a long, slow swallow of the rum drink. Ice clanked against the glass and bumped his lips.

"I believe I might wish for a lifetime filled with this nectar." He paused slightly, and then said, "Dude."

"Duuuude," Adam replied, drawing the word out to become a sound of affirmation. He raised his own Tiki glass and went back to his reclining chair. The deck was set high at the back of the house and, though the property wasn't actually on the shore of the Pacific Ocean, it afforded an excellent view of the sea and the coastal sunsets. The djinn moved about a little and finally settled on a wide lounge chair. A bit of smoke swirled about and he shrank down from his height of eight feet to a more manageable not quite seven. Following Adam's example he leaned back in the reclining chair, letting his feet rise with the bottom of the netting. Soon, faint snoring sounds came from his parted, ruddy lips.

The rest of the afternoon passed before the djinn awoke. There was noise coming from inside the house. The lamp still lay on the picnic table, imperfectly reflecting the grape-cluster-shaped party lights now casting a purplish glow on the darkened deck. The djinn picked up the lamp and stood swaying from side to side, gently and irregularly. His mission was still unfulfilled. He had not been commanded to do anything. He had also not been pulled back into the lamp. He had no idea what would happen if he did not grant three wishes, but found himself pondering the implications. No wishes, no returning to the Masters' realm.

Stars twinkled faintly. The light from the nearby city flooded the sky and gave the nighttime a whitish illumination. Traffic noises and neighborhood sounds traded comments. The djinn looked through the patio doors into the well-lit kitchen. Adam and an older man walked about carrying plates and cups and food from long counters to a round table. Two women worked with food and pans. One poured beverages from odd shaped jars. The djinn did not know what to do exactly.

Adam looked out just then and saw him standing.

"Hey dude! C'mon in. The Mom made some excellent grub for you."

The djinn walked inside.

"You are 'The Mom'?" the djinn asked.

"Dude, The Mom has a name."

Even at his now reduced height, The Mom still needed to bend her head back to look up into the djinn's face. "Call me Annie, please." The Mom's voice was fluid and friendly. Adam clearly favored his mother in complexion and hair color, but stood tall like his father.

The older man now approached the djinn, smiling. "I'm Kendall. You can call me Ken." The Dad wore his longish, thinning, dark hair pulled back in a short ponytail. He reached out to shake the djinn's hand. There was a moment of awkwardness due to unfamiliarity with current customs, but the djinn seemed a fast learner and hands soon clasped. Adam watched carefully. No sparks flew about.

Adam cocked his head indicating the fourth member of the family. "The Little Sister is Kari and she doesn't believe me about you."

"Right, you live in a lamp. Whatever. Bad sunburn you got. That's going to be painful tonight. I'll get you some aloe gel." Kari swept away with a tray of drinks and a full pitcher. Her hair, more the color of her father's, was also drawn back in a ponytail, though much longer. The family did a little more pre-dinner set-up dance, but soon it was time to sit down to the meal.

"Here you go, dude." Adam indicated the chair next to him and the djinn sat. A casual flurry of plate passing ensued and the djinn was served helpings of everything by Kari and Adam, who flanked him.

"So, Adam tells us you haven't decided on a name yet. You really can't remember yours?" Ken spoke politely. The idea of a genie from a lamp eating grilled salmon and couscous with fresh vegetables at his dinner table didn't seem to bother him at all.

"There have been times when Adam had the same problem." Kari cast a jibe toward her brother.

"Dude-*ette*, I'm done with that and he's not like that. It's more legitimate in his case. He hasn't used his name in a long time. Like you and your brain."

Annie interrupted the squabble before it got the chance to grow. "It would be nice if we had something to call you, but don't rush just to please us." She reached over and patted the djinn's hand. He sat quietly, observing the food and conversation and now looked down at the hand Annie patted.

"Dude, aren't you hungry?" Adam asked around a mouthful of food.

"I have not required food or fluids for so long. I do not know if I can be hungry." He took a fork full of salmon and placed it inside his lips. The djinn's eyes slowly closed as he let the flavor flow across his tongue. A slight smile and his eyes opened partially while he took a fork full of the vegetables. "I seem to be able to be appreciative of marvelous flavors." He dug in and soon his plate was empty.

"I believe I might wish for a life such as you have, Adam." The djinn spoke to the entire table. The family became quiet and looked at him. Annie spoke first.

"That is a very nice thing to say, Mr. Djinn. Thank you." She was genuinely moved. A slight tear hung in the corner of one brown eye.

"You are welcome," the jinni said, gazing long at Annie's face. "Gratitude is a stranger to me. I have not heard that sentiment in many years. Most people do not thank me for what they ask for." He spoke matter-of-factly.

"Well, we believe that gratitude is also sorely lacking in this world, so we try to make up for that lack in our household. It is not always easy, but effort made is never wasted." Smiling, Annie offered him seconds and the djinn readily refilled his plate. He raised his utensils and continued eating.

Nineteen quiet minutes later he wiped his plate clean with a bit of a sourdough dinner roll. He looked at each member of the family and purposefully said, "Thank you. Each one of you. Thank you."

"Well you are quite welcome. Any friend of Adam's is a friend of our family. I made up the spare bedroom for you. You do sleep in a bed, don't you? I mean, if you would rather sleep in the lamp..." Annie's voice trailed off. Her eyes spoke the remainder of the question.

"I do not actually live in..." The djinn started to explain, then changed his mind. "I believe I would...appreciate a bed. Thank you. Again." He paused, but kept his eyes on Annie. She smiled. To the djinn, it seemed Annie smiled often. He said, "You don't seem to be...surprised, by a djinn amongst you. Is the presence of one of my kind more common than I might believe?"

Kari giggled. "Well *if* you are a genie in a *magic* lamp, then we might be a little amazed. But you are in Southern California. We see crazier stuff all the time. Heck, we can go to Disneyland and see the Aladdin show. *That's* a funny genie."

"Kari," Kendall spoke sharply, but he did not yell. "Where is your energy right now? Do you really want to put..." no name was available, "Adam's friend down like that? You do not know what he is going through right now."

"Well, I'm locking my bedroom door tonight. That way I know what he won't be going through later."

"Kari!" Annie said, embarrassment crossing her tone.

"Kari," her father said, disappointment in his voice.

"Dude!" Adam said, a strange intensity pressing out at his sister.

The djinn raised his hands for quiet. "Little Sister Kari is correct. You do not know me at all. My very appearance is strange. It would be wiser to not trust me. Yet you have allowed me access to your home and even fed me. Adam offers me friendship. Now you offer shelter as well. It is unwise on your part, though well appreciated on mine. It is everything I could have wished for…" A strange look came across his face. "You have granted me three wishes that I did not know I had. You have done this in a way that I could not have asked for." He turned to Adam. "Master, if you have no immediate need of my services, I would like to spend some time under the stars."

"Dude. No need to ask. I'll check on you in awhile though, okay?"

"As you wish."

The djinn's exit left an odd vacuum at the table. The family finished their meals and cleared and cleaned dishes in contemplative quiet. Kari and Kendall left to their room and office respectively. Adam and his mother stood for a while in the kitchen, finalizing the settings on the dishwasher.

"If he really is a djinn, you need to be careful." Annie was not looking at Adam when she spoke.

"Not careful, mom. Wise." Adam sighed and looked toward his mother. She turned to look at him, their brown eyes mirroring each other. "I'm not sure I believe it either and I was there. 'Polish the old oil lamp,' you said, and suddenly red and orange smoke is everywhere. He's all like, 'I am the Jinni of the Lamp! I am here to grant you three wishes! Choose wisely!' and I just wanted to get him to quiet down and not wake up old mister Wilson.

"I don't do wise, mom. I'm a little scared here. What if I wish for 'peace on earth' and all the humans disappear, or equal rights for everybody and we all turn into factory workers. I could screw this up big time."

Annie slid her arms around Adam's waist and hugged her son. "Listen to you. 'Peace on Earth' and 'Equal Rights.' You're thinking about everyone else. Most people would be thinking about how much money to ask for, or what kind of car to command to appear. We haven't always seen eye to eye, but right now I am so proud of you."

Adam laughed and hugged her back, pressing her face into his chest. "Eye to eye. Good one, mom." He released her and they stood close. His hands rested on her shoulders while she lightly held his wrists. "We have good things now, mom. What else could I ask for? Life could be easier, I'm sure, but really, this is good right here, right now. What should I wish for?"

"I don't have that answer and even if I did, I don't think giving it to you would be the right thing to do. You've always tried to figure things out on your own and this is one of those times when you need to do just that. Maybe ask your father for some advice, but the answers aren't outside of you, Adam." She tapped his chest and smiled. "What does your heart say?"

He leaned down and kissed her forehead. "I'm gonna talk with dad."

The hallway was not long. The house was square, a remnant of old beach-town California, before the crowding of the late sixties and the last part of the twentieth century. Kari's door was ajar. Ear buds firmly in place, she nodded rhythmically to her private music while drawing cartoon characters in a sketchbook.

Adam's room was across the hall, dark except for the faint glow of multiple LED's shining from various electronic devices. One door further down from Kari was the door to the family office, wide open as always, and with Ken sitting listening to some jazz or blues from the sixties or fifties. His family had owned the house nearly that long. During his life Ken made several decent land investments. Not enough to be rich, but enough to have enough. His headphones stuck out from his ears, giving him the look of a giant mouse. No little ear buds for him.

Ken saw his son and immediately pulled the headphones off and set his book aside. Adam recognized the little yellow volume titled, *The Art of Peace*. The faint sound of Art Blakey's "Nica's Dream" rose from the headphones. Four large leather chairs populated the shelf-lined room. Low tables nestled each chair. Lighting was indirect for the most part, but there were three floor lamps at strategic locations around the room. One lamp shone a more powerful, direct light on Ken. He reached back and clicked it off when Adam took the chair next to him.

"It's about wishes, isn't it." Ken made a statement, but implied a question.

"What if I get it wrong, dad? It wouldn't be the first time, you know, in case you hadn't noticed." Adam gave a self-deprecating smile and stretched his legs out away from the chair. Ken mirrored his son's movements. He looked upward at the ceiling before beginning to speak.

"Failure is a teacher. The more mistakes you make, the more things you try, the more chances you have to succeed. The stakes are potentially higher here, but only if you raise them. The djinn seems to be...more normal than I would expect. You have that effect on people. You get them to slow down, think about things. Get a new perspective. The djinn seems to appreciate you. Don't betray that. The *Tao Te Ching* says, 'The Sage has no heart of his own. He uses the heart of his people as his heart.' What is in the djinn's heart? Help him fulfill that desire first and then observe your heart."

Adam rubbed at his temples. "The Tao also says, 'He who knows he has enough is rich.' Dad, I'm not going to ask him for anything, I mean like stuff, you know. Cars and money and stuff. Are you okay with that?"

"We didn't have a genie this morning. Our situation was just what it was and we were dealing with things. 'Stuff' doesn't necessarily make life easier."

Adam rubbed his palms on his legs and stood up. "Thanks, dad." The words were casual and common. He said them many times before. He stopped moving towards the door. Turning back to his father he looked him directly in the eye and said, "Dad, I mean it. Thank you for everything. Thank you for my life. It is a good one."

He walked out of the office and took a step down the hall. Kari was waiting for him, leaning against her door frame.

"Hey. Sorry I dumped on your friend. He really seems alright, for a big red smoky guy anyway." She shrugged a little and ducked her head. "I heard what you said to dad. The end at least. You're alright too." Kari hugged him, slightly higher than The Mom, Adam noticed, and then popped back into her room. Adam smiled and walked through the dining room and out the patio doors.

The djinn sat in the lounge chair he had previously occupied. In the night sky, the lights from airplanes floated about. A helicopter circled a nearby traffic incident.

"Are there no dragons to be seen anymore?"

Adam pulled a reclining chair over and sat down near the djinn. "Dragons, dude? No such thing except in stories, as far as I know."

"How far do you know, friend Adam?"

"Not too far, I guess. That's the first time you called me by name."

"Your mother, father, and your sister all called me, 'Adam's friend,' so I believe that you have made a reality regarding your name."

They sat quietly for a while. The quarter moon sank toward the western horizon. The night was cool, but the djinn sent off shades of subtle heat from his form.

"Adam, you wish to ask me many questions. I cannot read your thoughts, but I can sense moods. It was always this way with my kind, whether of the Ifrit tribe or Marid. I am of the Ifrit, the tribe of the smokeless flame. My wife, my partner, Measerah is…was from the Marid tribe. They are of the waveless waters. We were not typical in this bonding, for what does fire have to do with water?

"Part of my fate lies in my questioning of Iblis, once the leader of all djinn tribes. He chose a path that proved to be unwise. We djinn had free will in those days, but he expected us all to follow him to destruction. Many did just so. They challenged great beings by questioning their higher perspective." The djinn gazed upward and spoke matter of factly.

He turned to look at Adam and said, "There are powers and beings beyond your vision, friend Adam. Though I did not rebel against them directly, I was still djinn and thus, by my association with Iblis, suspicion hovered about my family and friends. As I chose to speak for us, they chose to deal with me directly. 'Why did I not act in opposition to Iblis?' they wondered. I had chosen a peaceful path of non-compliance. It is what I believed they, the ones I call the Masters of the Lamp, would have wanted. They chose to favor me with life as a servant rather than banish me from conscious existence along with the rest of Iblis' followers.

"The few of us that were left to exist were given this task: Serve others by granting their wishes. Does such a servitude have an end? I do not know, but I have come to believe that the answer is no. You offer me a different thought, friend Adam. What if the wishes were mine? What if free will were returned to me, and my powers remained? The question is one that brings the concept of great responsibility to my mind. The human Masters of the

Lamp have rarely felt such responsibility towards their fellows. I believe you will be a far different master.

"The power has limits. No one can be returned from the dead. No one can be made to feel affection or hatred for another. The wishes have a limit of three and no more. A wish for more wishes is a wasted wish. The power is also linear. I cannot make time reverse or return someone to a previous time. I cannot undo a wish once it has been granted. Remember these rules when you finally make your choices. I cannot interfere in your decisions or counsel or warn you. If there is excrement about to hit the fan, then I can do or say nothing.

"Before you make your wish I would like to say one more thing. You freely granted me your name. It is a powerful thing. You have been careful in your choices regarding your identity and the results are enviable. You are a work in progress and you are aware of this. Such self-awareness also is a sign of power. Continue to shape your destiny in this way and you will live a fulfilled life.

"My name is returned to my mind. You call me friend. As your friend, I am called Caphriel.

"I am also jinni of the lamp and you are the lamp master. In this, then, I am your servant and not your friend. This thought brings me deep sadness. I have enjoyed your friendship. Though brief, there is much power in our time together."

The moon set. In the ambient light cast by the coastal city, little starlight penetrated down to the earth. Masses of cars still rolled the freeways. Roaming groups of people still broke the night air with inebriated laughter or frustrated cursing. Autos seemed to be misplaced with frequency. Alarms seemed to be set off with regular futility. Dogs warned of dangers, mostly imagined, or barked their concern at being separated from their alpha human.

Out on the horizon, the ocean tide pressed in and out from the shore as it had done for longer than life itself existed upon the planet. Adam suddenly felt very small.

"Caphriel." Adam tried the name on his tongue. "Caphriel, what if I wish that we be friends? What if I wish that we be friends and then there is no 'Master of the Lamp' stuff? Just you and just me and the rest of the world is waiting for us to experience it however we want to. And 'friends' doesn't mean we have to agree or live together or anything like that. It just means we have a drink and a meal sometimes and keep in touch, share some time and talk and support each other when we're bummed or celebrate when excellent things happen or even laugh at each other if we do something boneheaded. What if that is my wish?"

"That would be a different type of wish. You do not want great wealth? Great power over others? You do not want all your enemies slain? You do not wish to be worshipped or be the leader of all peoples? You only wish to have me as a friend? You are an unusual human, friend Adam. I must say that you seem to have fulfilled your own wish, for already I consider us to be friends."

"Maybe I'm from the Ifrit tribe too."

Caphriel laughed. "You are not red enough."

"What if I wished that you live a good life? What if I wish that we have great happiness or that we bring great happiness to others? If I make that wish, do you retain your power? Do you become…I don't know that you are not human, but do you become human like me? What can we do, you and I, that will make the world better? Or, if we can't do for others directly, how do we make life good enough for ourselves so that we can benefit others?"

Caphriel pondered Adam's words before replying. "You say 'we' as if I have a say in the matter. The wishes, the commands, are yours to make and mine to fulfill. You propose situations that are complex and foreign to me. If you wish these things I must obey, but you are asking me if I *want* to obey. For many aeons the answer to that question has been 'no' and I confess I have been careless in fulfilling the commands given. Why should I, a djinn, obey humans? The wishes requested have not always been fulfilled to the full benefit of the human Masters of the Lamp." Caphriel paused in thoughtful memory. Then he chuckled a little, low and slow.

"Dude, that laugh sounds a little evil."

"I must say there have been times when I wondered if I have become a villain. I try to believe I merely allow consequences to occur." He sighed. "I wonder if I would retain my power. It would be a knife edge for you. There are three wishes. If the nature of your wishes are as you propose, I would experience a level of freedom I have not known since the days when the Weavers of the Veil were young. It would allow me to act in accordance with my own will, yet be under the rule of the first command. I could effectively grant random wishes at my personal whim. By your command, I would have to do good things and make happiness happen at my discretion." The djinn was not talking to Adam directly. He simply mused aloud and allowed Adam to listen to the thoughts. For his part, the young man sat quietly.

The djinn sat back. He looked at Adam and smiled. Chuckling again, lower and slower, he said, "You are clever, Adam. If we are to be friends, then as long as I exist so must you. If we are to be happy, you must remain healthy. If we are to do good things together, we must be well supplied. It is a way to ask for everything without asking for anything specific. I do not doubt your motive, my friend, but it appears that in being self-less you can gain much."

Adam stayed silent.

Caphriel continued, "You want to do good so you create good for those around you and for yourself. I wonder...what if this wish had occurred centuries ago? What will the future be like if we do this now?"

Caphriel looked Adam straight in the eye. "This too is a source of my imprisonment...my service. I once wished that everyone exist in harmony and seek the benefit of one another, regardless of tribe or type of being. I believed in it enough to resist an uprising and potentially lose everything. My family supported and shared my belief. It seemed as if we did lose everything, but...what if we were given these powers to fulfill such a wish?"

In the darkness it was difficult to tell, but Adam thought he saw smoke wafting from the djinn's eyes. "It has been a long time since anyone asked me what I believe in. I feel now that I have failed myself. I have not asked myself this question and I find that I do not know what I wish. I appear to have lost my belief.

"You create a world of possibilities for me, friend Adam. I fear that we may fail to make things better, but I also fear that we may not try. I have not been asked to take responsibility for my own actions for so long; I do not know what to do. Given a wish, a command, I know the steps and the way is easy. You have offered me potential and thus, responsibility. I must now weigh my ability to respond." Caphriel clasped his hands together and bent his head in thought. The night became silent. The two friends sat together in the dark, pondering.

Toward morning the sky darkened and the land lay in the longest shadows of the distant eastern mountains. There was no wind. The sounds of humanity were at their most quiet. Time seemed irrelevant and there was little to frame existence. The tide stood still and the ocean went unnaturally calm. Waves lessened and the water flattened. The two friends could hear each other's breathing. Neither one slept, though both dreamed.

"Maybe it will always be that people are in conflict." Adam's voice was soft as smoke. "Maybe it is because we are in conflict with ourselves internally. Maybe we cannot change the world. But, if we can visualize the image of a society without conflict, why can't we reach it? If it is a vision inside of so many beings, why can't it happen?"

The sky brightened as the sun crested the mountains. The house stood between them and the rising star and thus they remained in shadow as the morning progressed.

Adam rose and stretched. The sound of his joints popping broke their personal silence.

"Caphriel, I bet you wish that you had something to drink."

"There you go granting wishes again. That is supposed to be my task to you. The truth is, I find I am in need of some sustenance, friend Adam."

"Come on in the kitchen. The rule of the house is the first one up makes the coffee. I'll show you how." Adam led the way back into the house. "'Make the coffee' also means heat up water for tea or cocoa. Do you know these drinks?"

"Tea is familiar. I am eager to try coffee and cocoa. Your family seems to have the best food and drink available."

"We'll make some toast and honey too, but if anyone wants more they can get it themselves. My morning altruism goes just so far."

Kari's voice sounded at the doorway from the hall. "Your morning altruism doesn't usually start until about noon." She looked up at Caphriel. "So are we rich yet? Do we rule the world?"

"Is this what you would ask for, Little Sister Kari?" Caphriel spoke in very low tones.

Kari narrowed her eyes and pressed her lips together tightly. After pondering the question a moment she said, "Is that a trick question? I can see that this whole proposition is a tricky one. I'm glad Adam got the wishes. I might've just wished for Becca Fredricks to puke on herself at prom and that jerk Kyle Rodgers to wet himself right after that. Would you do something like that? I mean, if I had the wishes?"

"I thought that you didn't believe I was a real jinni."

"I didn't say I believed. I'm just, you know, exploring the possibilities, like theoretical stuff, you know? Anyway, I really wouldn't do that. I'm glad they found each other and I didn't have to go out with him to learn what a jerk he is. So, what wishes have you granted? Anything I might have heard about? Did you like, help Hitler come to power or something?"

"That wasn't me." Caphriel spoke very seriously. Kari's eyes went wide and she fell silent. She busied herself with making a cup of peppermint tea, adding liberal doses of honey.

Adam broke the silence. "Dude." His voice drew the word out. "*That* is a chilling thought. I don't know if you are serious and I'm kind of afraid to ask. Did some of these bad guys have a lamp?" Caphriel simply looked away.

The coffeemaker finished dripping. The aroma flowed about the room. Adam poured a mug for himself and one for Caphriel. "This is Komodo Dragon. Pretty strong, but I think you'll like it. Careful, it is pretty hot."

"Heat is not an issue for me." The djinn held the mug up to his nose and inhaled deeply. "This smells wonderful!" Ignoring the warning, he drank several swallows.

Kari looked at Caphriel as his smile widened. Gathering some of her spunk, she asked, "So, does anyone ever wish for something good? Like for all mankind?"

"Not yet." The djinn dropped his gaze down to the swirling steam rising from his mug.

"So if a villain gets the lamp, then you are like the ultimate henchman. Share how that makes you feel." Kari stared directly at the djinn. He shifted uncomfortably.

"I do not have a choice in the granting of the wish, only in the execution. Some wish poorly. I confess my performance is less than perfect for such ones. Good morning, Mother Annie."

Bath-robed and tousled, Annie staggered sleepily around the corner into the kitchen. "Good morning, Mr. Djinn. Adam, what are you doing awake at this hour? Did you stay up all night again?"

"The only way I can do it, mom." Adam poured coffee into a smaller, pretty mug, and passed the potion to her. He poured hot water into a mug emblazoned with the portraits of The Beatles just as Ken rounded the corner. A box of Earl Grey tea was set next to the steaming water.

Ken, dressed in a neat shirt, open at the collar, and wearing a sport jacket, set a messenger bag on a chair and joined the discussion as he brewed his tea. One pant leg was tied back in preparation for a bicycle ride to his office. "A rare thing here, all of us awake at the same hour." He turned to Caphriel. "Usually it is just Kari and I. We're the early birds." The djinn observed the actions of the family in silence, sipping.

"I heard the voices..." Annie seemed too tired to finish her thought and pressed the pretty mug to her lips with both hands.

"So what would you wish for, dad?" Kari asked. "Adam hasn't made us rich yet, but he also didn't try to take over the world. Which one do you want?"

"Well, I pondered this a bit after I went to bed. I like my life. There isn't much that would improve things. Every time I thought about it I could only come back to the idea that a better world for my children and their children was an appropriate wish. Now, I'm not the one who knows how to do such a thing. We have men and women who are better leaders than I could be, so I believe I would wish for wisdom to be bestowed upon all the leaders of the world to direct them to help craft a better and more prosperous future for all peoples."

"Did you just say, 'bestowed upon'?" Annie looked at him with one sleepy eye open and one closed. "I think that I would wish for the safety and happiness of my children. I'm already pretty happy with everything else. Mr. Djinn, what would you wish for?"

Caphriel blew gently at the smoke over his coffee. It wafted about and dissipated. Without being asked, Adam offered more and the djinn held the cup out in acceptance. The fluid, deep, dark, and rich, poured from the glass container in a steady and controlled stream. The mug filled and Adam tilted the pot back, causing the flow to cease. The remaining brew swirled about in the bottom and Adam set the glass gently back on the burner. Caphriel looked at the full mug he held in his large hand. The steam rose in abundance with the addition of fresh, hotter coffee. It rose higher, but dissipated all the same.

"I wish that you all realize the fullness of your lives, the blessings that you all enjoy. I wish that you all clearly see how you have each created this reality for yourselves and for each other. I wish that the harmony you enjoy and the principles it is founded upon may spread throughout the world.

"Were I the Master of the Lamp, these would be my three wishes. As the Jinni of the Lamp, I would be hard pressed to find a way to grant these wishes. It is much easier to cause a physical thing to occur than an idea. It is much easier to spread energy when it is in the form of food or coin or supplies than to channel the flow of creative force into philosophy and conviction. This does not mean I should not try." A deep sigh of resignation pushed the steam away. "It does not mean I should have let go my ideals.

"I was angered by the actions of the Masters of Light when they removed me from my kind, separating us as if we all were guilty of Iblis' violent revolt. Only, they had a higher vision. I see that now, though I confess I do not understand fully. Perhaps, in the separating, we were being given motivation. Make the world a peaceful place, harmonious and balanced, and then we would be re-united with our loved ones.

"Sadly, I believe that we djinn were too proud of ourselves, too proud of our self-determination to gracefully accept our servitude. The Masters of the Lamp must have felt it necessary to test us, to insure we were untainted by the desire to rule.

"My resentment at my treatment by the Masters of the Lamp made me blind to my true responsibility and their true purpose. I realize now that I am not punished by my task. The Masters of the Lamp saw in me, and those that followed my professed principles of peace, an opportunity to extend the harmony they must possess.

"They gave us, each of the ones who refused to follow Iblis in rebellious battle, they granted us a near unlimited power to teach and display. I fear that I have failed in my task. I fear that my fellows may also have failed, for I see this world still in straits of struggle and strife. I see the glaring misuse of power in the leaders and the strange acquiescence to these actions in those who choose to be led.

"I am left to wonder if, after so many centuries, it is too late to implement these principles." The djinn hung his head for a moment then raised it again and cast a look around at the family. "Then I see you. I hear your convictions. I watch as you nimbly shift your thoughts from petty revenge to higher realization." Here he looked at Kari and smiled. She blushed so deeply that she nearly matched his red skin. "I see the humanness of you in this way. I see how far humans have evolved.

"I see the surprise and the concept of fear when faced with a great responsibility." He now turned to Adam. "Then I see the willingness to, not simply accept the new and the strange reality you are presented with, but to feed and nourish that reality. You offered me, the strangest of strangers, an opportunity and space to examine my very reason for existence. You offered a great gift, the gift of perspective."

Caphriel sipped at the coffee. "Annie and Ken, you are strong beings indeed. You allow your children to create and make their own way even though you do not necessarily agree. You trust your children's ability to trust or mistrust. You only insist on politeness and respect within that mistrust. You adapt to the strange things that they do trust. You trust that your training will be effective."

Caphriel looked at Adam and said, "I know now what my wish would be. I offered friend Adam my name. In my time, knowing another being's name was a power and we granted our titles to each other sparingly. I now offer you all my name, for I have a desire to have you all as friends. I am Caphriel. It once meant 'Messenger of Peace.' I would reclaim that name and seek to bring peace to all who possess the lamp now and in the future."

With those words, a ripple flowed through the room. Reality wavered. A glow of energy pulsed at the opposite end of the kitchen, a light that cast no shadow. A sense of fullness grew and pressed upon them all. Caphriel turned to face the glow. They all sensed a presence arriving. It was a presence that only the djinn could see. The human family could not see, but they felt its voice. The djinn placed himself between the family and the presence. He cast no shadow.

Waves of energy rolled through them all. Within the energy came information, like sound or sight, but more, deeper, penetrating their core essences. Kari covered her ears with her hands. Ken and Annie embraced their daughter and each other. Adam stepped forward towards Caphriel. Before he could reach him, the djinn was embraced by light and raised off the floor. Adam held his arms out, reaching for the jinni, but could not touch his friend.

From everywhere they all felt the thoughts arrive. For the humans, the energy took on a voice and words echoed deep within their minds. They heard the presence speak to the djinn.

"YOU ARE CAPHRIEL.
YOU ARE AN EMISSARY OF THE LIGHT.
YOU ARE A MESSENGER OF SOURCE.
YOU HAVE OBSERVED YOUR COURSE.
YOU HAVE WITNESSED YOUR LESSON.
THIS DISCIPLINE IS AT A CONCLUSION.
YOU ARE GIVEN NEW RESPONSIBILITY.
ACT IN ACCORD WITH YOUR STATED PRINCIPLES,
FOR THEY ARE IN HARMONY WITH OURS.
ACT FOR THE GOOD OF ALL BEINGS.
ACT ON BEHALF OF BALANCE AND GROWTH.
ACT WITH WISDOM GAINED FROM YOUR EXPERIENCE.
SEEK OUT WORTHY ONES.
GRANT THEM OPPORTUNITY TO GAIN A HIGHER PATH.
SHOW THEM OUR WAYS.

"WE NOW GRANT YOU THIS WISH.
YOU ARE RESPONSIBLE FOR YOUR OWN COURSE.
EXERCISE DISCERNMENT. CHOOSE WISELY."

The light and sound receded. The djinn floated back downward to the floor. His feet touched the floor and Caphriel stood for a moment before falling to his knees. His head nodded forward and his shoulders slumped. He would have fallen over if the family had not rushed to him and surrounded his sagging form. Adam arrived first and struggled with the djinn's great bulk.

Annie knelt behind him and put her arms around his chest the best she could manage, grasping the djinn in a hugging motion.

"Caphriel!" Kari was the first to speak. "Caph,' are you okay?" She knelt in front of the djinn, cradling his face while Ken and Adam braced him at the shoulders. Together they prevented him from falling over completely.

In the midst of the family, Caphriel began to weep. Real tears flowed from his eyes.

A gentle shower of compassion flowed around him.

"Caph,' it's okay."

"We're right here, Caphriel."

"You are with friends, Mr. Caphriel."

"Dude, like, it's gonna be alright."

With each utterance they felt physical strength flow back into his form until finally he leaned back and sat on the floor, legs crossed. A mix of smiles and tears still flowed. He began to laugh gently.

"Friend Adam, it looks like you may have received your wish, after a fashion. In this, the Masters of the Lamp, the Enlightened Ones, show their wisdom. It is a wisdom that I now see clearly.

"Dude?" Adam cast a sideways glance at Caphriel. "Are you free of the lamp? I mean, I caught some of that bright light stuff but, are you your own boss?"

"It appears that I am indeed. And with some of the power still available to me to grant favors. I do not know the limits, but I sense that it may be a random thing, based on motive rather than duty. It feels pleasant saying that." He leaned backwards until he was lying outstretched on the kitchen floor. The family sat in the small spaces that remained. Kari held the djinn's large hand.

Opening one eye, Caphriel turned to Annie. "Is the offer of the spare bedroom still open, Mother Annie?"

"Yes, of course." Annie smiled and replied with no hesitation. "I wish you would just call me Annie."

"Wish granted," said Caphriel, and they all laughed quietly.

"You mean we have our own genie for a houseguest?" Kari seemed delighted and skeptical at the same time. "Do we get a flying carpet too?"

"Alas, Little Sister Kari, some legends are untrue," Caphriel said. Kari screwed up her face in faux vexation. The djinn quickly added, "I hope that I will not continue to disappoint you." Kari smiled then, looking much like her mother.

Caphriel sat up and the family gathered in a circle upon the floor.

"What was that Caphriel?" Ken asked. "Are we allowed to ask?"

"That was an encounter with the ones I call the Masters of the Lamp. In truth they are beings of great light, or that is how my kind perceived them. They exist on a higher plane; you might say a different dimension."

"Are they…" Annie looked back to the end of the room where the presence had manifested. "Are they angels?"

"In a sense, Mother…I mean, Annie, for they are messengers for a higher source of power still. But they have never asked for worship from my kind nor to my knowledge do they ask for worship from humans either. It is not a thing they need. I do not fathom their purpose.

"Their appearance to me and also to you is a rare thing. Encounters with them leave a being changed. I sense that you all have been imbued with some higher trace of knowledge this day. Of what use it will prove to be I cannot say. That will manifest when it is needed.

"The Masters of the Lamp, the Masters of Light, are often cryptic in their messages. It is up to us to exercise discretion and discernment in using their gifts to us. Once I failed in this. Now I am given hope again. Indeed, it was their final command.

"It appears that I am bound to Adam for a time. Yet this is not a binding of servitude. It is a bond of choice. My choice, but also Adam's. The Masters of Light heard your words, Adam. They discerned your true heart's desire and granted such to you. And I as well. It appears we will be friends by command as well as by wish. Perhaps Adam, you and I together, we shall find a new way to serve?"

Adam smiled and said, "As you wish, Caphriel. As you wish."

To Begin. Again.

Pressures

Potentials

Life, then LIGHT

Expectant explosion births event

Focus, then freedom. FLY

Profound space grants stellar place

Clouds collide. Emit…

Mites and motes hold hot steady flow

Quintessential elementals

Sequential helices

Circles, cycles, and vortices

Circuit clusters grouping galaxies

Scintilla of matter, glimmers, gathers

Systems form of orbits in courses

Stars spiral and spheres spin

And life, and life

begin

and begin

again

In the Meat

"STAND IN THAT LINE."

A warm glow emanated from the top of the man's head. It may have also come from his face and hands. In the bright white light of the vast space Ben found himself in, it became difficult to tell where the source of illumination came from.

"Why?"

"Why what?" The man looked up a mere fraction of an inch. His clipboard was white and the pages on it seemed whiter still.

"Why should I stand in that line?" Ben asked.

"Because it is your line."

Ben looked about. The room was huge. Upon reflection there was no real way to tell if it was a room. If there were walls, they were distant and the constant bright white made it impossible to gauge size. Only the lines of people gave any reference points. There were thousands of people. And they were all standing in lines.

"Why do I have a line?"

"Everyone has a line. It is what happens here."

"Where is here, actually? I don't recall deciding to come to this place."

"Very few decide to come here, but everyone does."

Ben felt something akin to confusion, but he was oddly at peace with the feeling. Nothing was normal, but nothing was wrong. He looked at the line waiting for him.

"If that is my line, why are those other people standing in it?"

The man in white sighed. Lowering the clipboard, he rubbed at the bridge of his nose. Finally he looked Ben in the eye. "They are waiting for you. They have your lessons. Before you can move on, you must hear what they have to say. They are everyone you met in the last incarnation and they will tell you what you did to them that they did not appreciate."

"My last incarnation? What, I'm dead?" Ben laughed. "And everyone I ever knew is dead too?"

"No." Another sigh and the man in white stretched. He hung the clipboard on absolutely nothing and it stayed. "They are not necessarily dead. They are not even the real people that you encountered. They are simply the energy of those people that connected with your energy at a certain point in gravity. That energy will appear to talk to you. You will listen. You can defend your actions if you wish. They will stay as long as you do. Now please, go stand in your line."

"So, I'm dead and this is heaven? If I have to talk to all these people that I ticked off, isn't that more like hell? I mean, is my high school class waiting to tell me everything I did wrong? Kill me now."

"Likely your school mates are waiting. You humans all seem to let that particular life experience affect you far too deeply. It is only four years..." He sighed again and continued. "You seem to have a shorter line than most. You must have been a nice guy." The man in white pulled the clipboard off the nothing and examined the list. "No time like the present." He took Ben by the arm and walked him over to the line.

As they walked, he talked. "Now you don't actually have to stand still. While you are in communication you can move about. Wander at will, but when you are finished you will find yourself back near the beginning of your line. Step up to the next person and begin again. If you move about you may find yourself in surroundings familiar to those where you knew the person to whom you are communing. You will not be able to interact with anyone but that person."

"So I'm a ghost."

"It would do you well to give up trying to apply the mythologies you grew up with. It is very different from what you were told. It is actually extremely different from what you are experiencing, but this is the closest situation we can attain that won't make your mental energy dissipate. You twentieth-century folks are not very capable of handling reality."

They were at the line and Ben looked at the first person waiting. She was young and cute and not really the way he remembered her from that summer back in the nineteen seventies. He thought maybe she was cuter than this, but vagaries of memory aside it was definitely Shelley. He smiled at the sight of her. She walked up and slapped him. Really hard.

Ben felt the urge to cry. He felt like he was lost and maybe he possessed no value. He felt like he was ugly or foolish or both. He didn't want to stay alive.

"I waited." Shelley spoke with a blistering intensity. "I waited every day for a letter. I asked your cousin about you. I wrote volumes in my diary and cried the pages wet with my tears. You *never* called. You *never* wrote. I was in *love* with you. You broke my heart!"

Waves of emotions pounded Ben's heart. He openly wept. He knew exactly how Shelley felt.

"I'm so sorry, Shelley. I really liked you, but we lived so far away from each other. When I went home after that summer I just fell back into my life."

"You entered my life! You made me feel special. Then, NOTHING! You left a big hole, a gaping wound, right here!" She struck herself in the chest with her fist.

Ben gasped at the pain. "Shelley, I didn't mean to hurt you. I didn't know how you felt, how serious..."

"I felt used. I felt like I was good for only one thing. What was special became a burden to me. I loved you and then I had to hate you!"

Ben felt worthless, cheap and immoral. He wished he could go back and undo...something. He was lost and felt alone.

"Shelley, you were so beautiful. We had so much fun those two months. I always remember that time as special."

"So special that you never once wrote a note or card or letter or made a phone call? I was damaged goods after that summer. I couldn't connect to anyone for years after you did that to me."

Ben felt vacant. Moments passed and they seemed like years. A daze, a fog of bitterness and emptiness dominated him. "Shelley," tears poured from his eyes, "I am so sorry. So terribly sorry. I was so selfish, so awful, and I did not even realize what you were going through. I was wrong and I would do anything to change it for you."

Ben wept a while longer. He'd fallen to his knees and his hands covered his face. Slowly the fierce emotions passed and he looked around. Shelley was gone. The line of people stood patiently at a distance. They gazed away from Ben and did not seem to notice him. He could not distinguish their faces. The man in white stood off a ways working his clipboard and talking to someone else. Ben pushed himself off the floor. He walked over to the man in white.

"Where did she go? Where did Shelley go?"

"You let her go and she let you go. She's gone."

"Is she dead too? She didn't die young. Why did she look so young?"

"She is still incarnate if that is what you mean."

"Then how is she here? What is this?"

"This is life. Well, from your limited perspective it is the afterlife, but it is all the same thing. One long string of complex energetic occurrences. No different than an amoeba or a galactic cluster. You just get to be conscious during it, that's all." The man in white looked Ben in the eye again. "Okay, let me try to explain. No one else here seems to need it, but I will indulge your questing mind.

"You are off the planet. What was your body is now decomposed. You are no longer incarnate, that is, you are no longer in the meat."

Ben patted his body. He screwed up his face in skepticism.

The man in white continued, "Your consciousness still thinks it is in the meat, but I promise you it is not. The people you meet here are merely the reality that you created from other people's energy. Shelley is still in the meat. You just met with her essence, the energy of her that you connected with in gravity. Get it?"

"So I'm dead."

"Do you feel dead? You are alive, but in a much larger way than you can imagine. You are in a state of continuance. Everything is. You are just out of the meat."

"Stop saying that! We're not just meat."

"That is what I am trying to tell you!" The man in white pointed with the clipboard. They were back at the beginning of Ben's line. The first figure started talking, loud and fast.

"Ben! What the hell happened to you, man?"

"Tom?"

"Man, you just vanished." A wave of loss filled Ben's chest.

A female voice echoed Tom. "Yeah, you were there for a while and then, poof! Vanished!"

"Zoë?" Ben wanted to be so happy, but another wave of disappointment pressed at his heart.

"Ben, we were close friends. How could you walk away from what we were?" A third voice came from behind Tom.

"Laurie!" She looked the same as she did in high school. He wanted to feel the love he had for her in their youth. Instead he felt battered and teary. Alone and lost, he did not know where to turn. He felt like running away. They all stood around him now. They did not touch him. When they were together in school, they always touched. Hugging, laughing, holding hands, their parents concerned that they were all too close, a tangle of teenagers who felt no boundaries. Now, nothing. It was all gone. No more closeness and this made Ben despair. Zoë took Tom's hand and Laurie shook her head, long blond hair delicately waving left and right. Zoë reached for her and then they were gone.

Ben wondered if he had blinked or somehow gotten turned around. He spun one way and then another. Always the line remained. He peered at the people, but could not discern the next face or any details of anyone in the line.

"Laurie!" He shouted and no one in line reacted. "Zoë! Tom?" He looked to his right, where the man with the clipboard seemed to be stationed. "Hey, White! Where did they go?" Ben staggered a little. The meeting with his three friends from high school left him weak. The man in white was swiftly by his side.

"Sorry, you four must have been very close." He dropped the clipboard and pulled Ben's arm across his shoulders to support him. "It is not often that more than one person approaches during this time. This is usually a private moment, one on one."

"Well, we didn't have many secrets. We knew each other inside and out. Why is this happening?"

"It is called the Empathy Pass. Everyone goes through it."

"Well where did they go? You said they'd stay until I let them go."

"I said they would stay as long as you did. It seems that you did not stay long."

"Will they come back? I want to see them again. I want to apologize, make them understand why…"

"This is not a place for apologies. It is a place for lessons. It is a time for review."

"What happens after this? How long will it all take?" Ben slipped his arm off the man in white's shoulder. He bent over, placing his hands on his knees.

"This is not a place where time really matters. Time is a relative thing and doesn't really apply outside of gravity."

"What the hell are you talking about? Do you have a name or are names relative too? Jesus!"

"Some want me to be Jesus, but here I am called Gaen."

"Here you are called Gaen? Where the hell is 'here'?"

"Well it is not actually a place. It is more a situation that is created by…"

"Forget it. Forget I asked." Ben stood up straight and looked about. "The lines, some seem like there are a lot more people in them than others. 'Relatively speaking,' does that mean people will be in this 'situation' longer?"

"Some take longer than others. Some don't seem to have had much interaction at all." Gaen gestured nearby.

A woman knelt weeping. There was no one in her line. She looked up and about, seemingly oblivious to Gaen and Ben's presence.

"Didn't anyone love me?" She sobbed out the words. To her left a woman in white appeared. Placing one hand gently on the sobbing woman's shoulder, she asked, "Did you love anybody?" Together they faded from view.

"You see?" Gaen said. He gestured again and Ben saw a long, looping line come into focus. "Now this line shows no signs of finishing."

Ben looked in awe at what seemed to be tens of millions of people waiting quietly to speak to the subject. "Whoa, what did that guy do that all those people are wanting to tell him off?"

"You know him as Adolph Hitler. It seems that he continues to affect people long after his death. He has yet to finish with those that were alive while he was in the meat."

"Six million and more…" Ben felt stunned. "My father fought in that war. He was pretty quiet about it most of his life. One day he sort of snapped. Dad got tough to live with for awhile."

"That is why you are in that line too."

And then Ben saw himself looking as he did in his late teens when all the trouble happened between him and his father.

Then he found himself back in his own line and there was his father looking back in anger.

"I hated your long hair. You just did not understand what it meant to me to have someone who didn't follow the rules. I always followed the rules! What did it get me? An ungrateful son!"

Disappointment flooded Ben. A sense of failure coupled with anger and beneath it all a fierce rage. A vision rose in Ben's consciousness. Men, his father's men, dying. His men died there and he could do nothing about it. He followed the orders to the letter and did not deviate from his command. They were overrun and decimated and they said it was his fault. His men, his brothers, perished because he followed orders and he knew nothing else.

His father continued, "Good people died so that you could have...what? Rock and Roll? Television? Howdy goddam Doody? What a waste!" Frustration balled up in the pit of Ben's gut. A feeling of too few options and overwhelming expectations clawed inside him. He grew angry with the failure of others and the absolute void of appreciation.

"I hated what you thought of me. I didn't 'sell out'! I worked for you to be free. I worked to give you options that I couldn't reach." Tears of rage turned to tears of shame. And Ben saw his father clearer, knowing the deeper motivation and tragic shame thrust upon the man. His father's tears became his own. He reached out and embraced him, weeping for them both and the lost opportunity to be appreciative of each other's lives.

And just as he did his father was gone.

And just like that he heard her voice.

"Your name is Benjamin Brian! Not just Ben! I gave you that name for a reason, the same as your brother. It was to honor your uncles and grandfathers and you just shortened it willy nilly." Ben smiled as he turned to see his mother. It was a sore spot with her and he should probably not be amused by it, not here, not now. But he was happy that this was the first karmic issue his mother had with him. If this was the main thing, the rest would be easy.

But it was not. It was simply the first in a long list of issues and all of them seemed petty and slightly ridiculous. Ben stood quietly listening. For a while he was okay with the litany. It was familiar and in this, somehow comforting. He soon grew restless at the meaningless nature of his mother's words. Detail piled upon erroneous detail. A desire welled up within his core to pick her comments apart, to press her for something serious or to just tell her to get over it all. Instead, Ben took deep breaths and, after glancing at Gaen and sneaking a peek at the line behind his mother, he simply kept standing quietly.

During a run-on comment about how he never really understood his loopy cousin and how he should have been more attentive to someone from the old neighborhood, someone that he actually did not believe he knew, his mother just seemed to run out of air. Her shoulders slumped and her head tilted forward. He thought she would deflate. Putting his hands on her shoulders in an effort to brace her brought him closer to her. Her head rolled back and she looked up at him. "No one ever listens to me! Only your brother. Only your brother listens. Not you! You're just like your father. You never listen."

And she was gone.

The next person in line spoke.

"She'll probably say the same thing to me."

"Chris? Christopher?" Ben's brother came into focus as quickly as their mother faded. "Did you hear any of that?"

"All the time. After you left home mom and I talked a lot. Well, mostly she talked. I just think that we grew up too fast for her. She was trying to figure out her own identity after dad got out of the service. She was so much younger than he was. You left so early and then really never came around, well, until later. It was just who you are. Or were." Christopher looked around. "Where are we exactly?"

"I think I'm dead. I don't think this means you're dead though. You just have to tell me what I did wrong in my life from your perspective, I guess. Can you see what's going on?"

"All I see is you. I saw you talking to mom. Heard some of what she was saying too."

"Jeez, that is kinda weird. I'm not sure you should be able to talk like this or see anyone else."

"He is following the flow of the Empathy Pass. He is just doing it in his own way." Gaen had appeared at Ben's side. Ben turned to him and back to Christopher.

"Do you see him? Do you see Gaen? He's...I don't know, an angel or something. Maybe a demon, but he seems pretty nice."

Christopher stood quite still. His eyes remained unfocused while Gaen spoke. "He cannot see me. He is suspended for the moment. When you return your focus to him, he will continue."

"What? He's on pause? Why are you here just now, anyway? No offense."

"None taken. This is the second time that more than one person has interacted with you. Very different. What is it about you that allows for such interactivity, I wonder? Well, press on." Gaen glanced at his clipboard and suddenly was no longer at Ben's side.

"Well, mom and I were always close." Christopher was answering Ben's earlier statement and Ben had to think hard about what the last thing he said to his brother was before Gaen had appeared. He couldn't quite recall so instead he carried the conversation elsewhere.

"So Chris, do you have anything to tell me? A complaint or some way I hurt your feelings or something?"

"No, not really. We were brothers. We grew up in the same house. After, I don't know, sixth grade maybe, you got your own room and after that I don't remember much of you or what you did. You and dad had some bad arguments. Pretty loud. Mom and I would sit together downstairs and try to carry on a conversation, do the dishes or something. It was like she didn't want to hear what you two were saying. Then you split for the coast. I was kind of jealous. You hit California and I was still stuck in school.

"Something wrong, something that I hold a grudge about? I got nothing. I thought you were cool for the most part. Mom missed you terribly. Dad didn't talk to her about you for a long time. I got him to talk, finally. He was pretty disappointed. I think he missed you in his way."

Christopher went on for a little while. Ben felt like his brother must have been carrying a heavy load. Thoughts kept rising within Ben. How could his father be different? How could his mother get ahold of him and not be angry? How could the situation be made better? And then he looked at Christopher and smiled.

"You did real good, Chris. You really worked hard to bring us all back together. I should have been more appreciative of you, but I just thought of myself, didn't I? You were a good brother to me even though I didn't see it. Thank you for that."

Christopher looked around again. "Well thanks, I guess. I just wanted everyone to be happy. So, do you suppose I'll be here soon?"

"I think so. They tell me everyone does this. It is called the Empathy Pass and I think you'll do just fine." Ben spoke the words, but Christopher had faded away.

Ben felt lonely then. He felt like all the people that should have been important to him had all left without a word of explanation. The empty feeling grew in his chest. He wondered about his own worth. Was he ever actually loved?

"Everyone loved you. That was the problem. You didn't stick around to receive or reciprocate." Madeline Pierson looked at him, cool green eyes framed by wild, flame-red hair. "I told you in our first session, 'No bullshit.' But you were really good at it and I missed it all. Until you left me too.

"I was a pro for most of my career. Then you came along. Your suicide attempt was real, but you were so likeable. I just fell for you. I went into complete mother mode, then slipped into lover. What the hell? What the *hell* happened to my professional ethics? And then you left! You left me just like you left everyone else in your life."

"Maddy, I left for your sake. I told you that in the letter."

"Bullshit! Ben, you left because YOU LEAVE! That is what you do!" The cool green eyes became intense. "A letter! After all we went through, you write a letter. What are you thinking?"

"Well, I think you mean what 'did' I think."

"DON'T! Don't you dare get semantic with me!"

All the questions of self-worth and reasons for existence came swirling about his mind. Why should he even continue this process? What if he just walked away from the line and went elsewhere? Did he have free will here? Could he somehow just stop the hassle of dealing with other people's emotions?

"I failed as a therapist. Because of you I lost all my confidence. I lost my heart to you. All my life, my job, my husband, everything went away when you left. And still I wondered if you were okay."

"Maddy, you know how confused I was then…"

"This is not about you, Ben!"

He resisted the urge to point out that it was about him. "Maddy, I am sorry. I was wrong to run off. We both know that I was in a wrong place all along. I wanted to get right and I knew that staying was just screwing up your life too. It was the right thing to do. It was all handled so poorly. *I* handled things so poorly. I am so sorry, Maddy. My feelings for you were true, but I was so unbalanced. I pulled you off balance too. For what it is worth, you saved my life. I had a decent life after that and you made a difference in a big way."

"Nice self-realization, Ben." Maddy smiled her Irish smile, pushed her hand through her thick hair and winked that wicked wink. And then she too was gone.

"Would it have been so hard?" Terri's voice came from behind him and it was *that* voice, the vexed voice, the one that told him he had not fulfilled her expectations. Rather, had not fulfilled God's expectations as she understood them. "Simple things, stay the course, honor the Father? I believed you when you made your promise to me, to God."

"Terri, you were eighteen. I was twenty. You just came out of high school. I was two years into college. What did we even know about life?"

"Then you left. I knew you would. I always knew that. My mother told me you would leave. Just like my father."

"We were together for ten years! I was nothing like your father."

"I never had children. I never had what the other girls had. Why couldn't you just have worked in construction like their husbands did? Why couldn't you just build a house for us to live in happily? All that talk about 'your art' was silly."

"Gaen! Can you put her on pause?" Ben said loudly.

"I only observe. You do the pausing. It all proceeds at your pace." It was true. Terri stood quite still, eyes gently unfocused just like Christopher's had been.

"Gaen, this is impossible. We had this conversation over and over when I was…" Ben struggled with the phrase, "in the meat. It never went anywhere. I cannot apologize for my life, my growth. I can't and I won't!"

Gaen pursed his lips. He may have been annoyed or simply pondering. He did not look at Ben directly. "This is the Empathy Pass. It is not the Apology Pass. You do not need to apologize. Not to anyone. If you choose to do so, let it be a result of the empathy you experience. You are not here to defend your life."

Ben looked back to his once-upon-a-time wife. He *had* been feeling defensive. Now, he thought about her words, her life. The insecurity she expressed, the search for approval from men, the need for acceptance by a group of people. Suddenly he saw her as a little girl, the way he'd seen her at the beginning. He felt bad about the lost innocence. He felt anger at the abandonment by her father, what it did to her and, subsequently, to them. Then he felt the worst feeling of all rise to the top, the sense of a talent wasted.

"Terri, you were such a good singer. I always loved when you used your voice fully. People loved to hear you sing."

"Yes, well now I sing for God." Ben felt her desire for approval from a father figure and he watched as Terri faded from view. He thought that he heard her begin to sing, an inhale perhaps, but then, no song came. He felt so empty and angry. He wanted to cry, but felt that might be wrong. He couldn't see the right thing to do. The frustration was unbearable.

"GAEN!" Ben shouted.

"I am close enough. No need to exert your energies in shouting to gain an immediate audience."

"I want this to end sooner than later. You said that this is just a perception, something that works for me. But this isn't the way things really are, is it? There is a more efficient way to do this, isn't there?"

"Well, we could go to a pure energy approach, but I really do not think you will like it. I do not think you can take the starkness of actual reality." Gaen's tone sounded a bit arch to Ben. A gentle challenge seemed to be included in the words.

Ben set his jaw and, leaning in close, looked Gaen in the eye. "Do it. I can take it." With those words the white room slipped away.

Ben found himself in nebulous form. Shapes and no shapes morphed and oozed near and through him.

Vast masses pounded against him. Keening pitches sounded in his sight. All things swirled. He felt rays of light touch his every element of being. He heard waves of energy pulling apart every cell, every molecule, every single sub-atomic element of his essence. Piercing light opened him, sliding through every fiber he once thought solid. Large spirals pressed him, taking his power and replacing bits of his core being.

Reduced to basic energies, his consciousness recognized no reality remaining with which to cling. Triple-helixed beings enveloped him. He was no longer a him. There was no barrier, no boundary separating what was once and could never be again. No eyes to limit true sight. No ears to stop the music of the spheres. No mouth to shape limited realities. No mouth to scream, yet he must.

He focused his fragmented consciousness. He reached out to find the essence of himself before it was lost completely to the raging energies of the Source of all things. The being that was and now was not Ben stretched to find itself. He searched for limits to accept. He created lines and membranes to hold himself back from the coalescing primal creation force. He sought the clean white light he had left amidst the fierce penetrating Overlight of the Mass of All. With one great last effort he plunged all his being into the single act of realization.

A rush like a storm wind carried him. A vortex of light pulled him from the radiating powers into a funnel, a gravitational well. He passed through the narrow end and dropped to the floor. The once bright light of the white room now seemed dull and flat as he rematerialized, on his hands and knees, back where he started.

Ben made a noise. He thought he was screaming. "Gack." It came out like a simple cough. He tried again. "Eck." His own ears registered the waves of vibratory movement of air. No one would have heard him beyond a few feet.

Gaen stepped up beside him. "Are you ready to continue?" Ben knelt. He waved a hand in a vague gesture that Gaen took as a yes.

Without further preamble, a woman's voice touched his eardrums.

"You kept crying. I felt sorry for your mother, but the plane ride was made very difficult because you were so fussy." And Ben recalled how his ears hurt during that flight. He could picture the interior of the airliner and hear the loud roar of the jets. He felt his own fear and terror. He wanted again to wail his pain against the unknown.

"I'm sorry." He spoke low to the woman. Straining to look upward at her from all fours he leaned back so that he was on his knees. She faded from sight when he said, "I was an infant."

Ben found the strength to stand again. The line continued and Gaen stood nearby, never interrupting, never interjecting, always looking from the clipboard to the line and making marks on the surface, never explaining. People appeared and faded after saying what they needed to say. Ben felt waves of anger, disappointment and, the greatest surprise, fear. There were some people that were actually afraid of him in his life!

As the line wound around there seemed to be more incidental moments, things that Ben did not even consciously recall.

Like, "You cut me off at the corner of Virginia and Elm! Absolutely ruined my day, made me late for work and got me written up and lost my promotion. Asshole!"

Also, "I was just trying to make a living! You jerked me around on the phone until my boss saw what was happening. He chewed me out and I couldn't get back in the zone. It was just a sales call! You could have said you weren't interested or just hung up!"

Or, "I messed up that order, but you didn't need to jump down my throat about it. You made me so nervous after that I was always afraid you would dump on me again."

And, "You were capable of so much better work. All the teachers wanted to see you apply yourself more. You could have been a brilliant artist, if only you disciplined yourself."

Ben felt numb at his core with all the people who felt somehow betrayed or at the very least disappointed in him and his life. Then, the line was finished. Ben felt empty. Empty and angry.

"Is that it? I screwed up everyone I ever met? I just annoyed and disappointed and pissed people off? My life was one big prickly shrub and anyone who got close got stuck? Why now? Why do I have to know this now? Couldn't you have told me earlier? Like sometime in grade school? If you're a guardian angel you really suck at it. You couldn't just say, 'Hey Ben! Stop being an asshole to everybody!' You couldn't have sent me a note or a message or a divine white light with a deep spooky voice inside? Christ! What a waste!"

Ben paced about during the rant. His left hand would raise and lower in a spasm of ire. His right hand would clench into a fist and pump the air in front of him. His head would tilt forward and then drop chin to chest in sudden jerks.

All the while, Gaen stood quiet. When Ben ran out of steam, the man in white simply waved the clipboard about indicating the rest of the white space around them.

Many lines remained. All were filled with people waiting. Ben drew a breath.

"Why?" his voice softer, tears in his eyes. "Why, Gaen? I did the best I could. I know I failed people. I knew it then, but I didn't fail everyone, did I? Was I really that awful of a human? Is it all too late? Or is there some Jimmy Stewart movie redemption that you can offer me?"

Gaen stood with his arms relaxed at his side and said, "First, I am not an angel. I am not trying to earn my wings. Not any more than you are. Second, what is done is done. No going back."

"We either get it right or wrong and that's it?" Ben asked.

"There is no right or wrong, Ben. Only consequences. Third, you are not done yet." Gaen pointed behind Ben. Ben turned around and saw the line had formed again. At the head was Shelley.

"Gaen, how many times do they tell me what I did wrong? Is this hell?"

"No right. No wrong. No heaven. No hell. Only consequences, Ben. Only life. Stand in that line please."

"Why?"

"Because it is your line, Ben."

With no enthusiasm, Ben turned to face the reformed line. It began again with Shelley.

"That was the most fun I ever had, Ben. I missed you terribly, but those two months that summer...well, nothing ever lived up to them. I cherish every memory of the time I spent with you. Every kiss, every movie, every walk in the park, and all the times we found that little shady spot. Ben, if I never had that time my life would be so much poorer." Shelley reached up and kissed him deeply. He felt the rush of their young love, the crush and passion of exploration, and the sheer boundless joy of two beings completely at one with each other. He kissed her back.

He recalled the end of the summer. Their constant companionship began to show their differences. Once content to be together no matter what, they started to have opinions and then differences of opinion. He saw clearly the future, and she did not. He returned to his home and found no reason to stay in close communion with Shelley. She too, did not write as faithfully as promised and soon time passed far enough that two months became a short time.

Shelley and Ben still held each other, but now they pulled away slightly and looked into each other's eyes. "Thank you, Ben."

"Thank you, Shelley." And he really meant it. The wave of gratitude washed the old patterns of youthful intimacy away then and Shelley faded from his arms.

He was immediately surrounded by Tom, Zoë, and Laurie. Laughing, hugging, touching or tickling, they made little puns and pulled jokes on each other. The conversation was random and wild. "Remember the time we…" "I liked when you…" "Wasn't that the day when we went…" "You made me laugh so hard when…"

Zoë and Tom separated from Ben and Laurie, wandering away. Ben and Laurie just kept talking and none of it was of any real consequence, but all of it was wonderful. Then they were alone together, just like it had always been.

"You formed me," Laurie said. "Everything afterwards, all my life, I compared to those days we spent together. Every summer day, every school dance, every time we skipped and went to Chicago, every single day was my touchstone for happiness. I know how different our lives were after school. I went away to college and Colorado was so far away. I thought about us all the time, but it was all so new in Boulder and I just got caught up. Then I just kept going and we never got back. I felt guilty about not being sad, but somehow I knew you were okay with it all. And the memories, the memories are all happy, Ben. I loved you then and I loved you all the way through to the end. Thank you."

Tears streamed from Ben's eyes as Laurie faded from view. "Thank you, Laurie." The words formed in his heart, but he wasn't certain that he expressed them aloud.

"I suppose it was too much to ask of you." Ben turned to see Terri standing to his right. Her voice was still vexed, but softer. "You were only twenty. What did you know of life?" Ben looked at Terri and said nothing. "You stuck it out longer than expected, longer than my father did." It always goes back to her father, Ben thought, and his own father rose to his mind. "If God forgives you, I suppose I can too." Terri's last words sounded musical, but that may only have been his imagination. She faded. No smile. He always loved her smile.

"I always loved your smile," he said, but there was no one there.

Ben turned to see if the line formed elsewhere. Christopher stood next to him, on his right.

"We never really got to know her." He was looking at the space where Terri stood just seconds earlier. "It was all a part of your life out west. It took us all by surprise, the religious stuff I mean. The wedding was nice enough, but mom was disappointed that she was not included more. Mom always wanted a daughter."

A woman's voice came from Ben's left side. He turned and saw his mother standing there. "You told me she made you happy. That was good to hear. I wanted my baby boy to be happy. Did you have a happy life, Benny?"

"Yes. Yes I did, mom. You gave me life and I appreciate it."

"I didn't understand your stories, Benny, but other people seemed to like them well enough. I didn't understand you either, but I always loved you. You know that."

"I know that, mom." He kissed the top of her head and she smiled and faded away.

His father stood in front of him and reached out with both arms. Ben did not know what to do. He could not recall being hugged or held by his father. Ever.

"You always made those funny little drawings. I kept them at my desk at work. It helped me remember why I put up with those people in the office. I wish I had done better for you, Ben. You seem to have followed your own heart and I admire that. It is why I wanted to retire early, get some of the traveling in that your mother and I talked about when I returned from the service. I'm sorry that you were gone before I could make that happen, but you were already out west and successful. I was proud that you were strong enough to do that. Thanks for making the little cartoons for me even if I didn't seem to appreciate them at the time."

"Dad, I…" Tears flowed, stopping his words. His father reached inside his shirt pocket and pulled out a little piece of paper. Ben saw that it was laminated. His father held it up for him to see. It was a drawing and Ben recognized his own childhood style. A man colored in blacks and grays held the hand of a little boy with a yellow shirt, purple pants, and green hair. A clumsy script below the two figures said, "You and Me."

"We buried that with Dad." Christopher's voice came from the right. Ben wept so hard that he failed to notice his father was gone. "He was proud of you, Ben. In the end, he was proud. You did what you wanted and you did good things. You made people happy, Ben. We didn't get it all the time and sometimes I think you didn't get it either. You were a good brother, I mean, when you were around. I wish you'd been around more, but I loved the times you were there." Christopher pulled Ben close and held him tight. Together they cried until they laughed.

They laughed and Christopher left. Ben turned to Gaen and smiled. "Sorry for all that stuff about being a bad guardian angel and hell. I didn't understand."

"You can go pure energy again if you like." Gaen also smiled, but his tone was wry. "It will be a little easier from here on."

"No, thanks, this is fine. In a way it is harder than the Empathy Pass. Embarrassing really."

Gaen looked at the clipboard. "Yes, you never really took a compliment well."

"I just did what I did. I didn't do anything for reward. Well, maybe a little, but not in big things, you know."

"Nice for the sake of being nice? Goodness as its own reward? Is that what you mean?" Gaen asked.

"I guess so. I never really spent a lot of time thinking about the philosophy behind it all."

Gaen looked at Ben and nodded. "I will endeavor to remember that." Ben started to ask what he meant, but Gaen spoke first. "I have some more people ready for you. Are you ready to continue?"

Ben had been wiping tears away during the break. He took a deep breath and said, "Well there can't be too many more, right?"

Gaen gestured with the clipboard and Ben turned around. Jonny the spiller walked up and shook his hand.

"Thanks, Ben. I was the fat, messy kid in school, remember?"

Ben recalled Jonny quite well. Many times he'd dodged erupting sodas or Vesuvial condiments. "I know you, Jon. It's good to see you."

"See! You were always nice to me even when the other kids were making fun of me. Do you remember Carla? She had the locker next to you?"

"Carla?" Ben's memory was fuzzy on this one, but he smiled anyway.

Carla stepped up to Ben and took his hand from Jonny. "I was so nervous all the time. My family was overprotective. I was not prepared to deal with so many people in school. You were always nice to me though. You helped me learn how to get around and how to use my lock. It made things easier. Thank you."

Jonny spoke again. "Remember Arnie?" And Ben did remember the little guy. People used to pick on him because of his size. "You let me walk with you out of gym class so the jocks wouldn't pick on me. Thanks. Maria Gonzalez is here too."

"You never made bad comments about me being from Mexico. You helped me find a book in the library. Then you showed me what the teacher expected for our assignment. Thank you."

Jonny brought more people forward, many from school, some from jobs Ben had when he was young. Most were unconnected from Jonny, but he seemed to be the leader of the group. It seemed to go on for hours and no one left. They all stayed, gathered around Ben. Talking with each other and sharing their lives before and after the little moments that intersected with Ben's. There was no line, just a big group, and they talked of moments where they were able to do nice things for strangers. Some cited Ben as setting the example. Most did not and Ben thought they would've done those actions anyway. They were all good people.

Time passed and the group scattered and wandered away, their images fading or disappearing in the milky distance of the white space. Jonny stood in front of Ben.

"Jonny, I don't know where we are, but it looks like you have some ketchup on your shirt. Did you really spill on yourself in the afterlife?"

Jonny laughed. "It is how I was when you and I were together. I went into the army after school. I don't know if you knew that. I became a medical officer. Went into the field, triage stuff, saving the wounded soldiers. I died trying to pull a kid out of a burning truck." Jonny placed a finger right on the red spot that Ben thought was ketchup. "Sniper bullet to the chest." He snapped his fingers. "Me. Gone. The kid made it. Went back home and had two girls and a boy. Named the boy Jonny. He looked up my own son and they became friends."

"It sounds like you are proud of your life, Jon. It sounds like you did good things. You had a son?"

"Called him Ben!" And Jonny shook Ben's hand as he faded away, smiling.

The line reformed. It was mostly strangers. "Thank you for opening the door." "Thank you for carrying the heavy groceries." "Thank you for helping me with my wheelchair." "Thank you for the donation." The litany of appreciation flowed on until the line was nearly at an end.

Ben heard a cat meow. He looked down and saw a little black cat, then a second and a third. A little gray and orange tortoise shell walked up with a striped tabby. A dog walked up too and Ben recognized the little mutt and all the other animals. They all rubbed against his legs or wagged tails or mewed or purred. Some he did not even remember as his pets. Ben knelt down and scratched ears and petted backs and rubbed tummies as the animals clambered all over him. One by one they left too. Ben lay on his back, eyes closed, a blissful smile on his face.

Gaen made a throat-clearing noise. Ben opened one eye and looked up. Gaen stood still, waiting.

"More?" Ben asked, incredulity embedded in the word.

"One more," Gaen said.

Ben sighed, stretched, and stood slowly. He looked around and saw no one but Gaen. The man in white spoke. "You connected with all those people. They all were better because of the little things you did. I will try to remember that, even though I know I must forget the reasons why."

"Forget? It is all on the clipboard, right?"

Gaen hung the clipboard near to Ben. There was nothing on it. No marks. No words. No paper. No pictures. What had Gaen been looking at all this time? Ben looked at Gaen with a question in his eyes.

"It is my turn now," Gaen said. "Keep track of everyone I interact with while I am in the meat. When I come back, you will be in charge of my line."

"Why me?"

"Because it is your turn." Gaen appeared to be transparent.

"Wait! Isn't there an instruction manual?" asked Ben.

"None that I've ever found!" Gaen smiled.

"How will I know what to do?" Ben's hand reached toward Gaen's arm. It passed right through.

"How do we ever know what to do?" Still smiling, grinning actually, Gaen faded from sight.

Ben felt a subtle vibration. He felt lighter and realized that, up to that instant, his body carried a density. Now it felt as if his very structure loosened, that the atoms moved farther apart. He felt transparent, as if he were attached to nothing. He felt released.

A glance down to see if he could actually see himself made him see the light. Gentle and white, it emanated from his form. He appeared to be wearing white clothing, just like Gaen. There was no judgment in the next thought, only observation.

"I don't think I care for a double-breasted jacket." The jacket shifted and altered. "I prefer the shoes lighter, not so dressy. Canvas deck shoes perhaps. No socks." And it was so. "No tie, open collar. Pleated pants with a cuff, looser all around, and a thinner belt." He smiled as everything happened just so. He found that he was dressed like Gaen, but also like himself.

Ben started to put his hands in his pockets. It was a casual stance, one that he was well known for. Nearly every picture ever taken of him from the time he was a child until adulthood showed him that way. His right hand slid easily into the loose, wide pocket of the trousers, but his left hand held something.

It was a clipboard. Like Gaen's.

Ben looked at the item. No paper. No pen. Only an image, a man and a woman in a moment of deep intimacy. It seemed wrong, at first, to witness such a thing, such a moment of privacy, but Ben saw the act in a different way now. He saw the deeper energy of the passion, the heat of life itself. He wondered why this should appear on the clipboard. He observed the climax of the moment. The clipboard showed him clearly the face of the woman.

Ben pulled his right hand from his trouser pocket. Reaching inside his jacket's inner pocket, right where it always was, he drew out his favorite pen.

Next to the picture of the woman, Ben wrote, "Your mother smiled."

Last Words

THERE ARE NOISES IN LIFE THAT HAVE MEANING. We use language and words to express our innermost thoughts and emotions. Sometimes though, the words, once full with meaning, become mundane and empty from common use.

They may be true at some level, but they have become rote, ritualistic, and lack the depth they once possessed. Terms like "thank you," "see you soon," "miss you," "lovely to see you again," and even "love you," accompany the leave-taking of family and friends from gatherings, dinners, or holiday parties.

That night we said those words, all of us, and they meant something, but they were not deep. Not nearly deep enough.

Ken and Karen were in the midst of the swirling noise and then they were gone. To all of us there they simply ceased to exist. Word did not even arrive until two days later.

Ken and Karen were meant to depart early the next day, a black limo whisking them away in the wintry dark

Midwestern morning to the airport and the summery sun of the island resort. They had saved for this trip for two years and it was to be three weeks of warmth, sand, wine, and no responsibilities, before they returned to business and set to building a family.

On the day following Christmas, two days past the party, the phone in the hallway rang. I believe that I knew the call would be difficult before picking up the old-style receiver. The sound of the ring seemed to be reluctant, as if the telephone itself did not want to bear such news.

"Gone," they said. "Ken and Karen are gone," and it was a natural thing for me to laugh and ask, "Were they delayed in departure?" My words were flippant, without depth. My question thoughtless.

It was not that they were delayed, but premature in departure, departure from this world, and I choked on my laughter and my meaningless words.

A car slides off the road in darkness and ice. A car plummets down a long steep hill in the depth of night and snowfall. A car is covered and buried by the fresh white that we all rejoiced in on Christmas morning.

Of all the words we can say, we rarely get the meaning right at the right moments. What I wished to be my last words of love to Karen then, my final thoughts of appreciation to Ken, my admiration of their resolve and conscious course to make a fine and better life, now hung in the empty entryway festooned with the wreaths and ribbons, only one day past their purpose for existence.

The elements, unkind from our perspective, left their physical remains in a state that dictated closed caskets, our final images mercifully were of Ken and Karen alive and flushed with the warmth of fire, family, and friendship.

I choked and wept and in this way communicated my grief to my partner and spouse. "Gone," I said, wishing the one who had communicated the news to me had themselves been wrought with a similar emotion, giving me the clue I needed to prevent my foolish laughter.

We took each other in our arms and clung together. For hours we stood and sat, fetched water and tissues for each other, searching for the right words and finding none. Our emotions went unvoiced, but we communicated them nevertheless.

We could not bring ourselves to see the big picture, the randomness of life and events. We sought deeper meaning and found only an emptiness that words, meaningless words, could not fill. We were deep in our emotions and our hearts, and felt the pain of sudden disconnection and loss.

In our heads we spoke of the process of loss and the stages of grief, but we could not remain inside of that place of logic and reason. Our anger spread about and never settled upon any one thing.

That evening we prepared for a sleepless night. I looked at my chest, expecting fully to observe a deep purpling bruise in the area of my heart. Of course there was none, but that made me angry again. Why not? I wondered. Why could I not take the damage in a physical way? Let time heal me from a physical blow to the heart. It would take less time and be less painful.

Tomorrow, work beckoned, but we already talked of the day and knew we would not be at our desks, our offices. Our absence from the workplace would mimic our loss of friends and family. Our employers would understand. The loss of family, especially in such a tragic way, and at the holiday time too.

"So sad," they would say.

"Yes, take the day off. We can handle things here," they would offer.

"Our thoughts, our prayers, are with you." They would speak the words that were meant as comfort and we would feel the emptiness.

The office would endure our absence, but we would return.

In the dark of that night I recalled the old prayer my grandmother taught me.

Now I lay me down to sleep.

I pray the Lord my soul to keep.

If I should die before I wake.

I pray the Lord my soul to take.

I felt only anger at the lord of the prayer. But I feared the third line and the meaning of the words.

I bolted upright in bed, breath rapid, body shaking. My partner asked if I was alright. We said words then, deep words and meaningful words. Precious thoughts and emotions that we carried inside and did not release in mundane days. They were the same words that previously had lain empty on the foyer floor, only now, this time, we infused them once again with meaning.

Thoughts of life, emotions of love, and in the deep night we resolved that others must know of our love for them. We lit candles and pulled paper from drawers. We set our hands to the task and the words came and lay upon the paper. We knew then, as dark turned to late winter morning light, not to waste our words. Not to waste our moments of life and existence.

We thought back to the last moments of Ken and Karen, before they ceased to be a part of our future. We remembered saying "I love you" and "We will miss you," though at the time we did not know how badly.

We remembered being the first and only ones to know of the third member of their family. We had promised to stay quiet about the baby until they returned and were able to make a formal announcement. We vowed to keep this promise now.

Our lives would not be the same. We will be saddened in years to come, especially at the time of the holidays. But we refuse to be pressed down and away from joy in life and we will not fear the future.

The next day we invited those that were in attendance that last time, the last night we all were together. All arrived save Ken and Karen.

The gathering was an imperfect replica, a reunion in memoriam, a party with no hope of gaiety. We raised glasses and told stories. We ate leftovers and said our goodbyes to Ken and Karen. We spoke of our love for them. We wept. We spoke of our love for each other and wept more.

At the end of the evening we all met again at the door. The words this time were the same as before, but different. We thought as we spoke. We purposely sensed the meaning behind each "thank you," each "see you soon."

We did not hesitate to speak the words "I love you" and we did not hesitate to feel the full meaning of the words. We wept the words until grief turned to joy.

I love you.

Life will become routine again. We knew it then and know now that it has done just so. On occasion, a sadness will seep into our hearts. Perhaps, we will wonder, perhaps we should have remained in mourning just a while longer. Then we will hear within our hearts the last words Ken and Karen spoke before they departed.

"Thank you all! You are the best friends we could ever wish for! Have fun while we are gone!"

AUTHOR JEFFREY J. MICHAELS combines fantasy, science fiction, and humor with metaphysical elements.

This is his first widely distributed selection of short stories. His intention is to suggest alternate approaches to life and living. And to make you smile.

You can visit him at www.jeffreyjmichaels.com to learn of his current projects.